MESSALINA

Messalina

A NOVEL OF IMPERIAL ROME

Alfred Jarry

TRANSLATED BY JOHN HARMAN

First published in **La Revue Blanche,** in 1900

© 1985, Atlas Press
All rights reserved
ISBN 0 947757 07 4

Published by Atlas Press, 10 Park street, London SE1
Printed by I.P. West One, Heddon street, London W1

British Library Cataloguing in Publication Data:

Jarry, Alfred
    Messalina: a novel of imperial Rome.
    I. Title II. Messaline. **English**
    843'.8[F]   PQ2619.A65

ISBN 0-947757-07-4

CONTENTS

THE PRIAPUS OF THE ROYAL GARDEN

THE LEGITIMATE ADULTERIES

THE PRIAPUS OF THE ROYAL GARDEN

I

THE HOUSE OF HAPPINESS[1]

Tamen ultima cellam
Clausit, adhuc ardens rigidae tentigine vulvae,
(Et lassata viris nec dum satiata recessit.)
D. IUN. IUVENALIS *Sat. VI.*[2]

That night, like many other nights, she descended from the palace on the Palatine in search of Happiness.

Can this really be the Empress Messalina, her supple body radiant in silk and pearls, who steals from the bed of Claudius Caesar and prowls wolf-like along an obscene street of the Suburra?

It would have been less surprising if the bronze She-wolf—that long, low, wry-necked Etruscan statue, ancestor of the City, and its guardian—had shaken from her unfeeling teats the puckered lips of Romulus and Remus, like one renouncing a golden crown, and leapt with one bound from her pedestal below the Palatine (opposite the ruminal[3] fig-tree beneath which the twins were found), to pick a path through the heaped-up filth of the district, her claws brushing the ground with the dry rustling of a heavily embroidered train.

Indeed, this form ranging through the city with crumpled train—or claws, is akin to a hunting beast, although unaccompanied by the reek of the She-wolf.

Has anyone ever smelled the odour of a statue on heat?

But this monster returning to her lair is more insatiable and infamous, yet lovelier, than the metallic female: for this is the only woman to incarnate absolutely that word which, since the foundation of the City and since Latin was first spoken, has been cast in the face of prostitutes as an insult or a kiss: *Lupa*. This living abstraction is a more prodigous terror than any sudden vivification of an effigy on a plinth.

The oldest myth of Latium is again made flesh in this twenty-three-year-old woman: the She-wolf who suckled the twins, another form of Acca Laurentia, telluric goddess and mother of the Lares,[4] the earth bringing forth life, the bride of Pan—also worshipped in the shape of a wolf—and the prostitution that peopled Rome.

Coins before the time of the She-wolf bore a purer imprint: the fifth century *quadrans* carried the image of a sow.

But it has always been this She-wolf, the City's founder, that has ruled over it.

And now Messalina approaches the door of the *lupanar*, house of Happiness, where she knows herself to be more of an empress than in the palace of the Palatine.

Happiness resides, apparently, in one of the lowest brothels of the Suburra, crushed at ground level by the weight of six stories, as the pudenda grovel beneath the mass of the body. Buckets of ordure stand beside the threshold, and on either side are the crumbling establishments of the butcher and the public executioner.

The functions of these shops—for a shop is what it is—are only distinguishable by their signs. In the executioner's window a bloody whip is drying; the butcher has had a dragon painted on the lowered shutters of his shop, to frighten off the children who might piss against the wall and to deter beggars from unhooking the strings of sausages.

Between these undulating curves—the whip worrying at the night breeze and the painted coils of the serpent—and seeming straighter in contrast, there is something like a staff, but thicker, as though a flag were wound around it.

Its facade, to a passer-by of today, would simply remind him of a provincial police station, on any day but Sunday.

But the Thing is more monstrous, strange and enticing, for it has a meaning.

This divine and animal emblem, the great Phallus carved from a fig-tree, is nailed to the lintel like a night-owl to a barn-door, or a god to the pediment of a temple. Its wings are two lanterns made of yellow bladders. Its face is rouged in paint, exactly like that of Jupiter Capitolinus.

Above, legible in the lantern-light, the banderole of the cloth sign would flap in the wind were it not pressed by the rigid god against the wall, which is his belly.

She stands before the hanging *animal*, the Augustan whore,[5] flesh of deified emperors, disguised by a great cloak of deep purple, each of whose folds is a gutter for shadows—the star in the darkness of her hood is a blonde wig, for Messalina has dark hair. More goddess than Laurentia, she is like the Night herself, conjured out of the sky by the screech of the night-owl in its death-throes.

But this is only a woman who has noticed that her husband has fallen asleep.

Claudius Caesar has grown drowsy through over-devotion to Venus, but . . .

Is Messalina's husband never allowed to sleep?

A man is the husband of Messalina during the moment of love, and then

10

for as long as he is able to live an uninterrupted series of such moments.

Her only husband is he who does not sleep, and Messalina has come, in the lurid costume favoured by courtesans, and wearing a courtesan's scarlet ankle-boots, as though she were fording the bleeding life-stream of Claudius' exhaustion towards he who does not sleep, the god-beast, Man eternally erect, with a vigilant lantern on either side.

She has only one attendant, a notorius professional prostitute who surpassed her by a single figure in a love-making contest lasting a day and a night, by absorbing the twenty-fifth male.[6]

The empress has thought fit to humbly concede her defeat as a gladiator by granting the victor the privelege of carrying her train in the capacity of slave.

They penetrate the low door of the *lupanar*, warm as a vulva.

Within—the tremulous half-light of smoking lamps.

An empty corridor, two bare walls lined with cells, the doors closed —inhabited.

The Happiness which fills the house to overflowing, if one is to believe the sign outside, is meted out in smaller portions, according to the labels on the cell-doors.

There is indeed a measure of this happiness behind each partition. Behind each is a woman, or an adolescent, or a hermaphrodite, or a donkey, or a eunuch, according to the amount of pleasure which a mere man is able to enjoy.

A crowd of men is waiting. And just as the men make their selection according to the descriptive tickets, so the prostitutes will examine those proffered by the customers, in the circular form of silver coins—sestercius or denarius—which they use to justify their desire.

Their treasure of sesterces and their desire are kept pent up in a circular atrium. Beyond the wall separating it from the booths all is the feverish activity of the hive.

Only one cell is empty, that reserved for the queen bee, which the *Augusta*, the emperors wife, resembles—although here the label proclaims her *Lycisca*. Not a single lock of black hair protrudes from beneath the small helmet of false yellow tresses, the traditional colour for courtesans; she is quite naked now, her breasts tinted with gold.

Sometimes a tracery of golden thread weaves a heavy caress across her breasts, but tonight they rise and fall in freedom, the areolae smeared with a golden balm.

Her cell is as small as the most uncomfortable of modern bathrooms and as barely furnished as a lavatory; a deep stone bench, shorter than a body at full length, runs from one wall to the other beneath a red mattress.

Messalina lay down, and a man entered soon afterwards, she turned onto her left side, her knees together and drawn up against her body; the man's hairy legs, heavy with iron sandals, fitted themselves to the mould of her calves. When he bit the nape of her neck, she turned her head to the right to catch his tongue between her teeth.

Only then did she see his face and shoulders.

It was a soldier in a leather uniform and Messalina felt as if a living goat-skin bottle was overflowing within her.

Aroused now, she hastened the departure of this first lover. Immediately the cell-door swung open with a crash—the last dying echo of the bacchantes drum—and the streaming reek of the *lupanar* swirled through the smoking aperture. Just as a blood-red peacock would dazzle the eyes, an athlete, burnished with pumice—as if marble, knowing itself less beautiful, had taken revenge and become sculptor—sprang from a flying purple cloak, casting it aside with the habitual gesture of a net-fighter.

The lamp alone blinked, the black eyes of the blonde courtesan, incorruptible grapes, remained unaltered in the wine-press of the man's chest and the stone bed.

And she closed them in pleasure, her hard thighs forming a tight band around her adversary who crouched over her. But the courtesan's true eyes were more watchful than ever, the gilded tips of her breasts glinted with undying fire.

Then they illuminated a chariot driver of the Frog-green Guard; Messalina thrust back her hair down the wall, and as the gold-tipped boundary posts are crushed by the chariot-wheels, so she cried out, pierced by the chariot's ivory shaft.

And there came men, and men and men.

Until dawn, when the *leno*, or brothel-keeper, dismissed his maidens.

She closed her cell-door last of all, later even than her servant, still consumed with desire.

Outside, Messalina turned for one last look at the place where she had been happy for so short a time.

The image carved in fig-wood of the god of generation—the supreme god of the ancients since even the Father of the gods was dependant on him, *father* only by its favour; the emblem of universal life and the solar god —stood out sharply from the pediment of his temple.

And Messalina, before this idol, re-embodied the eternal myth of the amorous antagonism of the *She-wolf* and the *ruminal* fig-tree, that is to say the tree of fruitfulness.

But the house was closed, and the gross effigy of happiness seemed to be signalling to her from above the threshold, pointing out another path, and indicating that her true abode was elsewhere. With its cyclopean eye toward the infinity of stars, now fading away, as though Happiness increased with remoteness—had it just stabbed them out with the unity of its mouth and stare? The scarlet head strained toward the absolute.

And it seemed like a great bird stretching its neck, about to take flight.

Messalina did not leave the spot until the night sky, now in triumphal purple as at a sacrifice, put on its *pretext*[7] of dawn; and with a sputtering of animal fat the twin lanterns were extinguished.

A sputtering: Messalina saw, quite distinctly, the flight of the god in a strident clatter of unfurled wings. The rigid image in fig-wood of the god of the gardens had deserted both priestess and temple and vanished, no doubt towards more Olympian heights— as though this Immortal, flushing still in the ritual obscenity of its vermilion head and at having to prove itself more man than the other gods, now felt the need for a renewed deification.

Wherever it came to earth again would surely be the perpetual abode of happiness.

She returned to Caesar's bed. He was still asleep, for she had had the foresight not to summon the imperial concubines, anticipating her desire to be possessed one last time, and by the only man who had the right to love her *totally naked*. Messalina cast aside—somewhat regretting the lost finery, although her skin was still exquisitely defiled by the dirt and stinking fumes of the *lupanar*—the decorum of her golden wig.

II

BETWEEN VENUS AND THE DOG

Colitur nam sangine et ipsa
More decae, nomenque loci ceu numen habetur;
Atque Urbis Venerisque pari se culmine tollunt
Templa: simul geminis adolentur thura deabus.
AUREL. PRUDENTII *contra Symmachum lib. I, 219*[8]

Claudius arose when Messalina slept at last, and in the dawn light he entered the quadrangular, glass-paned study which rose above the terraced roofs of the palace—the belvedere built by Augustus. And this ludicrous and incomprehensible man—for history has been unable to pronounce him idiot or genius—dictated to his secretary Narcissus, as he had previously dictated: The History of Rome (in forty one books), A defence of Cicero against the Aspersions of Asinius Gallus, the Tyrrhenian Annals (twenty books, in Greek) and the History of Carthage (eight books), the following:

THE BOOK OF DICE[9]

THE MEMOIRS OF CLAUDIUS TIBERIUS NERO DRUSUS GERMANICUS BRITTANICUS CAESAR

'This work shall be read annually as a public lecture in the new museum which I have founded in Alexandria, and where my other works are taught; and may it please the gods and the name of Augustus that it proves more instructive than my history of Rome since its foundation. I must have been mad to attempt such a treatise. With my head nodding from left to right, I cannot even unravel the direction of my own destiny, **whether I am to be a king or a fool,**[11] Theoginus or Caesar!

'When the dice lies upon the table, it is impossible to decipher both the face and its reverse. The luckiest throw, the double six, is named for VENUS, and always seems to be hidden between the table, shinier than **her** marine looking-glass, and the ivory cube. Whereas the double one, the bankrupting DOG, appears again and again, with monotony.

'Oh gardeners with your thumbs harder than these cubes of bone! The sun is rising; fill up your little white baskets of twisted osier rushes with blue hyacinths . . . or perhaps with yellow marigolds—for though I was born on the first day of August, my eyes opened at the eleventh hour, when those flaming flowers of the Kalends bloom. You thank **Fors-Fortuna** for your pockets heavy with silver, and **Iacchus** for giving you drink; honour me by placing these bouquets before the palace of your Emperor!

'If the **senes**[12] of Venus seldom surge to the upper faces of the die, is it not because she is more woman than goddess and finds in the deepest beds her surest oceanic bliss?

'More woman? It must be Valeria Messalina, my wife. For she is very beautiful.'

'Yes,' said Narcissus, *who knew*, being Messalina's lover, as were most of the freedmen and the Emperor's *Friends*—a title that corresponded to that of courtier. And his blunt stylus did not pause in its laborious inscription on the wax. Claudius appeared not to hear.

'. . . But Messalina is my third wife; I repudiated the first, Paetina, because she was just an ordinary woman, committing minor crimes; then there was Urgulanilla, who had a taste for murder so I cast her out, followed by her naked daughter Claudia! Since I married Messalina I limp more with my right foot. Husband of Venus, " Η-φαισ-τος ! [13] both our names have an odd number of syllables which, according to Pythagoras, indicates a blemish on the dexter side.

'But by Vulcan! Was the master of the Cyclops taught, like myself, by a **driver of beasts of burden** rather than by a freedman versed in grammar? I never let him forget his past occupation and I fixed my eyes on his goad of a ferrule.

'My mother Antonia Minor called me an abortion and a rough draft of nature; and Livia, who was considered so intelligent that her grandson Caius called her 'Ulysses in skirts', could only fill her letters with insults.

'In reply I employed a little of my imperial divinity, and decreed her an apotheosis, on her death.

'As for Tiberius, he exempted only myself from his list of possible successors to the imperial throne.

'But he was prone to absent-mindedness, particularily in important matters. Adoptive son of the illustrious family of Julius, he forgot their mother was Venus, and failed to complete the temple of Venus Erycinus in Sicily.

'I restored and finished the temple of our divine ancestress.

'But before these events occured, timidly and with an affected and exaggerated imbecility, I passed my time in the taverns with the vilest inebriates; my nerves in rags, I drank . . .

'And my mother's cruellest and habitual insult was:

"He is more stupid than my son Claudius!"

"More stupid than Claudius!" She could have anounced it to the whole world as the philosophers' most irrefutable axiom, had she only known! There was neither genius nor king that was not a poor brute beside Claudius, asleep in the tavern and oblivious to the buzzing of flies—it was not I who snored!—and the olive-pits, thrown in derision. Here he was, after nights and days pursuing his only really imperial pastime—an ordinary citizen holding fate in his hand, in the form of the dice!

15

'When I rubbed my eyes with the women's shoes that had been placed on my hands as I slept, my confusion was more from the fading dreams than the awakening glare of the light. And when a feather was forced down my throat, I clamped my teeth on it as if on the bleeding mouth of a mistress, forcing back the gorge, shouting 'thieves!' for I imagined I was vomiting the hair of Fortuna!

'This life lasted forty-six years. At forty-six I was not even a senator. I had never been shown to the soldiers. But I saw a soldier later, then a great number.

'And since it was obvious to everyone that I could not comprehend the present, I was made an augur, and called upon to forsee the future.

'Waving my augural **lituus**[14] from east to west, in order to define the boundaries of the consecrated **templum**[15] and the farthest limit of my vision—for I am myopic and felt like a blind man probing with his stick all the deep obscurities of the heavens!

'And so, now that I'm the Emperor, I've not asked the Senate to swear to the inviolablity of my future acts, although this has been the custom since the time of the triumvirs.

'And yet it seemed no more unnatural to me than my limping right leg that, on the first occasion I appeared in the forum as a consul (where my first act was to play at checkers with Vitellius), an eagle swooped down and perched on my right shoulder!

'Fate consistently limping on the same side is . . . chance.

'Now, here's how I was elected by the Imperial eagle. When the conspirators slew Caius Caesar Caligula, I fled, paler than the Dog-dice, from the glare of blood and blades flashing with flames, I ran through the high vaulted gallery with slanting windows that joins the Circus to the palace. Hidden in the **hermaeum**,[16] my ill-omened feet—I think my head and feet must be the twin poles of a die!—protruded beneath a tapestry. I heard the scraping of the extraction of the first sword and as the empty scabbard slapped against the soldier's right thigh, I fell at his feet to beg for my life—my head trembled beneath the tapestry, animating its fringe.

'But destiny must have willed that this soldier, his steel raised, saw in the still invisible body crouched over its uneven feet, its head with only sparse white hairs, too long a nose and uncertain eyes—a being worthy of the imperial eagle! For the praetorian prostrated himself and kissed my knees that knocked together—from fright, no doubt, but also because it was my fiftieth birthday—and saluted me as Emperor.

'He called the rest, and they carried their Emperor in triumph to the camp beyond the tenth gate, the furthest from the enemy. They carried me—to the ringing notes of curved horns and straight trumpets—because I trembled so ·uncontrollably I could not walk.

'Good soldier! I was the first to buy the soldiers' allegiance with money! No more of these decorations fit only for adorning the temples of Mars and Honour: civic crowns, murals, valae, naval crowns, wreaths, **picus purus** (which are merely sleeves), tablets . . . I invented glory in kind, **decoration with gold!**

'Oh how long, thin and gangling I was behind that tapestry! Am I even certain I was concealing myself? Was I not rather veiling my head—so high!—for it is a sacrilege for a dead man to meet the gaze of a god?

'But, by Augustus! It is not I that is divine—apotheosis is a vain glory of shades. I live! My bones still harmoniously move the numbers on all their faces. It is Augustus who is in bronze at the end of the **Spina**[17] of the Circus Maximus, and he is veiled at every killing in the games. I remain a free spectator in my **pulvinar**; while he holds him-

16

self—or is eternally held by his divinity—more rigid than the corpses which are removed while still warm and pliable. For the bodies of common gladiators cannot be allowed to imitate the inflexible metal of the imperial statue. But, because I am merciful, I had his statue removed altogether, not wishing it any more tears. Besides, it became necessary to veil it too frequently.

'I believe—yes—that I am good. I do not allow the games to be restarted more than once on the same day, if there has been an infraction of the rules. The **bestiarii** now know they risk dying only twice daily.

'For I can afford to exercise my authority once in opposition to the desires of the people! I am very mild-mannered and humble; once, after a triumph, I crawled up the steps of the Capitol on my knees, my old knees that made me Emperor . . .

'But at least I was going up!

'Now they say my actions are clumsy and my speech is indistinct.

'But I know that I am a great orator.

'But what am I saying? Narcissus! Faithful Narcissus! Are you taking care to impress the whole soul of Claudius your Emperor upon the wax?'

And Narcissus read back impassively, and perhaps Claudius, in his dreaming, had dictated only this:

'Claudius the first, Sabine Attus or Attus Clausus, established himself in Rome in the year 250. He changed his name to Appius Claudius. The followers he brought with him formed the tribe of Claudia, as Virgil relates (En. VII. 706—709) . . .

Meanwhile, beneath the belvedere, Messalina awoke:

A little after the fourth hour, or as we would say ten o'clock in the morning, her maid-servants conducted her to her toilet.

This room was almost unremarkable. The stucco panels between the columns were blank save for various tiny designs gleaming in their smooth white centres, like decorative napkins arranged around a plate—their subjects: a lyre, a horn of plenty, a basket etc. But there was a tall narrow mirror of Sidon glass beside the window that opened onto a panorama of the city that included the western slopes of the Hill of Gardens. On the other side of the window, in a similar gold frame, was a full-length, life-sized portrait of Messalina, naked, executed in pearls save four points where rubies gleamed.

Scattered across the shelves and tables, depicted in various materials on boxes and vials of essences, powders, unguents and paints, and ornamenting their tops with lasciscous immobility, were the presiding statuettes of the goddesses of love: VENUS, COTTYTO, PERFICA, PREMA, PERTUNDA, LUBENTIA and VOLUPIA.

VENUS was absent, she did not mix with the six minor goddesses. Doubtless, she was the portrait in pearls.

The minor gods formed the handles of curling-irons, small mirrors, gold pins and bells for summoning slaves; their names—PRIAPUS, BACCHUS, MERCURY and PHALLUS.

The hair of the child Bacchus, each ringlet formed in the image of a grape-pip, topped the curling-iron, whose handle was a twisted vine-branch. The serpents of Caduceus entwined about a circular mirror, their writhing conformed to a double symmetry, like eels swimming across the surface of a pond, twinned by their reflections.

PHALLUS was missing. He should have been a carved gem, an extended pin, preciously imitating the great sign before the *lupanar*. But his mistress and humble worshipper had stamped upon it angrily on awakening, and thrown it out the window toward the distant green panorama. For she recall-ed, as if in a nightmare, that hallucination of the monstrous image taking flight in the dawn. The dawn that shuts the house of Happiness, extinguishes the lanterns and disperses ghosts and phantoms.

PRIAPUS was a coral toy which Messalina's delicate hand used to agit-ate a tiny silver skeleton, like those carried at festivals; it danced and rang at every joint. Now it was hung apart from the little bells with which she sum-moned her maids.

Messalina turned away from the great mirror—the first, last and most voluptuous bath—and rising out of this sea, with a glance absolutely devoid of jealousy at the other Anadyomena of pearls, she removed her own—that is to say she was dressed.

With her back to the mirror and the long window that stretched the entire distance between two stucco columns, she followed the motions of the hair-dresser's iron in two mirrors—in the depth of the little disk of polish-ed gold, which she held by the double servant, were the curls on the nape of her neck. And also, framed and constricted by the window, there were the terraces of Lucullus on the west slope of the Hill of Gardens.

The City and the Woman adorned themselves.

Now the dresser had ranked her hair with combs, and two heads were revealed side by side in the mirror, alike in appearance and scale. The hillside curly with plane-trees and ivy, decorated with coral, tortoise-shell and gold enamel; and the shock of Messalina's hair with its shining summits and sombre abysses, tufted with esplanades and beneath, red porphry trickled from giant urns over ornate polychrome colonnades.

And simultaneously, the diamond aigrette, the dresser's final touch, flashed in the southern sunlight and perpetual noon of the gold disk that mirrored both Empress and City, and the fountains on Lucullus' highest terrace blossomed with jets.

There is a cameo of Messalina, that was copied and preserved by Rubens, which shows something like this view of the city and the woman twinned in a mirror; the Empress, and behind her Octavia and Britannicus, her children, facing *Rome, helmeted*. The sardonyx is curved, and the two busts are like the two branches of a candelabra.

According to this cameo, and another of Claudius and Messalina guarded by two dragons, the Empress had a face of exaggerated fullness, round like a breast, or with something forcibly swallowed. The mouth is tiny but nevertheless occupies the entire face, for the jaw-muscles are powerful and would serve an animal; the nostrils wide like Cleopatra's, inherited from Mark Anthony, her great-grandfather—it seems as if this overpowering love had endowed the children of the legitimate spouse with the characteristics of the mistress. Not beautiful, in fact; but then the fire of her eyes has been put out in the unliving stone! And surely beauty is only a convention? Or perhaps a form that is called beautiful is but a *vase for passion*, and one preferably unblemished, uncracked even, as it is itself of the purest transparency!

Under the pale skin, in a froth of veins the colour of the sea, Claudius found Venus Anadyomena!

And he was not surprised that the Empress should compare herself to the city, as there was a parallel cult of VENUS and Rome. And Augustus had ordered that the cult of the City should always be associated with that of the Emperor; and Cato the Elder, consul, had erected the first temple to the City at Smyrna in 559. Twenty-four years later Alabanda had built the second, modeled on the temples of Venus, and the first Christian poets wrote:

> *Her worship is bloody, to her (Rome)*
> *As to a Goddess, for the place is taken to be a god;*
> *And to the City and to Venus, the temples rise to an equal height*
> *And incenses mingle together and smoke to these twin goddesses.*

And, as though admiring herself in the mirror, Messalina contemplated in her hand-glass the groves, tableaux of box-trees, carved yews, cottages and garden statues of Priapus less numerous than the pins in her hair and its gems.

Suddenly she burst into sobs, and in her room it was as though the great mirror of Sidon glass had shattered across the mosaic floor—a sparkling arena of powdered specular stone!—or as though the pearls of the portrait were unstrung and the beauty of Messalina flooded over the ground in a thousand fragments.

Something like the cry:

'Great Pan is dead!' [18]

She went to see him in the stable of the he-goats—Pan, Priapus, Phallus, Phales (his divine name), Love, Happiness, the god for whom she knew the greatest number of invocations. If he existed, he must surely be here, and not in the absurd statuettes, temple jewels and frail toilet utensils.

She saw him.

He is favourable to men, but briefly, and dies as soon as he touches a woman—Oh, the sobs of the Venus of pearls falling back among the grains of the sea-sand, *Katadyomena!*

And if he is revived it is only to die once more, like his image, the great nocturnal eagle perched above the door of the temple, which extingushed its flashing eyes, extended the span of its amorous pinions, and appeared to rise in the sky—in her imagination the nymphomaniac conjured up a more and more precise vision—and really fly away with the dawn in the same migration as the last flickering stars.

'Where are you Phallus, Priapus, son of Bacchus and Venus? It is your name alone that alters; where are you God of the Gardens? I think of you absolutely—my desire is certain and I am sure you have an existence independant of the stable saint and the dead discarded clothes of women.

'Jupiter, the father of the Gods, lives on Olympus and in his temple on the Capitol; likewise Augustus in his temple; Livia, goddess and my husbands ancestor, also inhabits Augustus' temple and wherever women swear by her name. But we other women . . . we other gods!

'For the wife of a deified Caesar is closer to a god than other humans! A god he may be, but Claudius has allowed the erection of but a single silver statue, and two of brass. He has forbidden the people from prostrating themselves before these effigies of the *Imperator*, the conqueror of Cynobellinus' city[19]—Camulodunum by the Thames, past the very limits of the habitable world. And the legions (the *Claudian,* the *Faithful* and the *Pious*) would not have penetrated these regions had not the eagles on their flagless staffs followed the feiry tracks of the torches in the sky, that auspicious Eagle of lightning!

'Eagle of Rome and the Suburra, have you then returned to extinction in the marshes of Britain?

'I am the City itself!

'I am *Augusta!*

'My husband will soon be deified; he is already fifty-eight years old.

'And I . . .

'Priapus, my fellow god, do not be vexed that my apotheosis is still so distant: god of love, it is because I am young!

'*God of the Gardens . . .'*

20

Lucullus' terraces sparkled under the high sun of the sixth hour, the Greek *pallia* billowed between the arches of the library portico, statues moved among the *xysti,* [20] the silver statue of Diana Persia was an effigy of the cow offered in sacrifice on the banks of the Euphrates by the builder of these gardens, beautiful as a king's. And its identity was indicated by the lamp which shone through the streams of water, light and crowds, like a fish at the bottom of a stream. The figure of Mithridates, six feet high and solid gold with a buckler of precious stones—a mirror for larks, splashed the whole Orient over the parterres.

'. . . GOD OF THE GARDENS! I understand your name for the first time, it identifies your abode: you inhabit *the most beautiful of all gardens!* For if your rough image, fashioned by a shoemaker with a knife from, perhaps, an old fig-tree, protects the stony enclosures of the poor, then the most perfect of all your representations, you yourself, O Phales, must dwell in the finest garden. The over-hanging foliage is the roof of the House of Happiness!

The Empress leant from the window of the palace and awaited the parting of the green veil of the temple and the revelation of the Virile Divinity.

But the foliage in two greens, plane and ivy, and the lawns of liquid acanthus remained as impenetrable as a mask with lowered eye-lids, or perhaps the City just turned away its head from this woman, whose head was large as Rome.

The Empress turned from the window in her turn, and the great City shrank back and stretched itself out flat in the serpent frame of the round mirror, like a medallion.

But then Messalina glanced into the mirror a second time, and she melted into tears.

With the same unhealthy certainty with which she had first read in it the province of her flown chimera, she suddenly deciphered the reason for the gods departure.

It was an ancient Latin doctrine that Rome had many names.

The vulgar name, *Roma*—means *strength* in Greek, and in Etruscan the Tiber was called *Rumon*, and it renewed the *ruminal* fig-tree annually— almost disclosed the name of the god to whom the City was consecrated.

As a child, Messalina had learnt from the vestals the sacerdotal vocative: FLORA.

But there was a secret and terrible name, which it was forbidden to utter on pain of death, for it was the actual name of the god of the City (the people were led to believe it might be VALENTIA or ANGEROMA).

The priests taught that on the day THE NAME was pronounced, the tutelary divinity would leave and go elsewhere to seek, as the sacred formula put it, *a more ample worship.*

And so, although the name was unknown, it had become customary, for fear of an unfortunate accident, to say:

'*The City.*'

It was the profane word ROMA that veiled the brows of monuments like a mask, when an inscription referred to the city.

And Messalina had just read the exergue of the medallion of the City in her golden mirror (but was so overwhelmed that her lips did not spell it out) it was the sacred name, scarcely suspected and never pronounced *as the name of the City* or the departed god. The dedication over the portico of Lucullus' library was reversed in the mirror:

$$\text{AMOЯ}$$

But when the Empress had wept like a rain over the gardens, they appeared so beautiful that she saw the god could not have abandoned them. She observed herself in the mirror, her face eclipsing the entire City, and she cried out loud, calling the god by his name, fearlessly:

'AMOR! god of Rome, thank you for quitting Rome and its stinking Suburra for the gardens that bloom beneath my window. You are no city-dweller; deck yourself with flowers, rustic god, eternal god of gardens! You will find no *more ample worship* than in your new domain, GOD OF MESSA-LINA!'

She returned joyously to the window.

'Whom does this City resemble, helmeted in a green wig, who would be a woman, or this woman who wishes herself City? I recognize you, though you hide your face! You are Poppea Sabina, mistress of Valerius the Asiatic, who bought these gardens for you to sculpture into a representation of your neck and hair. He paid as royally for this caprice as he pays your husband Cornelius Scipio to be a husband in appearance alone!

'The garden is very beautiful, and Poppea Sabina is a beautiful woman —though not as beautiful as I! Her dresses are made of a single piece of silk, embroidered with birds: unrolled, they are as long as the ambling line of the five hundred she-donkeys who supply the daily milk for her baths. Once I saw a marvellous ball of Sidon glass, large as the head of a man. It was discovered when my husband—who did not see the god—had all the bushes probed and searched to calm his usual suspicions. I have not so perfect a mirror in my toilet, except perhaps my portrait in pearls. Once I looked at the Circus Maximus through a Scythian emerald and, as in the mirror, objects close-to appeared greater and things at a distance were shrunk to nothing. I believe that it predicts the future. In it I saw tiny future wrinkles on myself and was delighted to find myself ugly.

'Then the reflection of Caesar's nose swelled and grimaced. A naked man would see himself as a god in that globe! The god I seek! But the glass ball, like a human head, is filled with nothing but vain dreams.

'The Asiatic must have brought it from Asia to present the god with a mirror! It is the conserved image of PHALES which gives it the virtue of reflecting men in the aspect of apotheosis. The god certainly favours the Asiatic, his temple priest. The solar god is first seen by the inhabitants of those countries where the sun rises. Now I understand why Poppea prefers the Asiatic to her husband, although Cornelius is handsome—I know as I have slept with him. I have been told the Asiatic is bald and fat and that his eyebrows are crooked! I have not known him, yet. If I . . . know the god he keeps in his garden—but perhaps he is that god. As I lock up my jewels, so will I obtain the key of the garden of the god!'

She extended her hand toward one of the images of Phales (there was scarcely an article that did not bear it on its handle) the most childish of her toys, the silver ringing rattle, whose substance recalled the imperious and imperial memory of clicking bones.

Calm, wanton, determined, she rang for a denunciator.

III

THE ASIATIC MASTER OF THE TREES

Sed truncum forte dolatum
. *Arboris antiquoe numen venerare Ithyphalli*
Terriblis membri, medio qui semper in horto
Inguinibus puero, proedoni falce minetur.
L. IUN. MOD. COLUMELLAE *De Re Rustica*
lib. X (De culti hortorum)[21]

The juidical denunciators had been created by Tiberius to transmit secret accusations directly to the Emperor. They laid their charges before the praetor in the presence of the accused, having already signed the allegations with their deputies. Tiberius' fragile tyranny found them very useful and he called them either *the guardians of the law*—for they were the instrument of punishment for its transgressors—or, by antithesis, the Eumenides. With gold and favours he coaxed them from the shadows as his needs dictated, like drawing a sword from its sheath; and this metaphor had become current, and the more ruthless of the denunciators thought of themselves as a naked sword ready to fall. The most naked, ready and dearest to Messalina was a certain Publius Suilius; it was he she had summoned to arrange the legal ruination of the Asiatic. He had once been a questor to Germanicus, but had been exiled to an island for accepting bribes.

In that most delicate part of the following day, the dawn, Messalina, contrary to her custom, did not fall asleep, but kept Claudius to his bed.

Publius Suilius entered the imperial chamber at the head of a disorganised mob rather than a troop of soldiers. They clamoured around him—and someone else—in confusion. The ivory bed was now a throne of justice, and the denunciator announced:

'I have here proof of the crimes of Valerius the Asiatic, and witnesses to them. I deliver this criminal to your mercy, O Caesar, he who has publicly proclaimed that he regretted not slaying Caesar with his own steel!'

On the bright white sheets Claudius' fingers, paler still, rattled and clicked.

'Those who first acknowledged you as their Emperor, and who you must treasure dearly (in that you provided them with their treasures), saw him rise to his full height on a hillock on the very day of Caius Caesar's death and cry out: 'Oh that it could have pleased the gods that he should have died by my own hand!'[22] And since that day, as they are all prepared to swear,

24

Valerius cannot ascend even a small mound without being taken by a mad frenzy to do away with an emperor. Now, there are at least seven hills in the City, but you, O Caesar, are unique!'

'He sought to corrupt us with the exotic profusion of his riches,' said a soldier, 'but we are loyal and cannot be purchased with gold or debaucheries, for now we are Caesar's.'

'He is preparing with an accomplice to travel to the armies of Germany,' said another. 'It will be a simple matter for one born in Vienna to enlist the aid of his numerous and powerful relatives on that first frontier of the barbarous East, and raise the tribes of those lands in revolt.'

'He is Poppea's lover, I believe,' whispered Messalina.

'Here are certainly enough words,' interrupted Claudius, 'and fate delivered her judgement the moment the accusation was pronounced prior to the defence.'

'Finally,' Suilius added, 'and to omit nothing, I saw him prostitute himself, counter to his sex, at the Circus. What may be legitimate for a youth is monstrous for this balding old man.'

And he pointed his finger into the crowd.

'Ha! Which bald old man do you mean, Guardian of the Laws,' sniggered Claudius. 'That is my secretary.'

Messalina's eyelids blinked rapidly, for the irregular but compact ranks of soldiers still concealed the Asiatic.

A vibrant voice spoke out, each syllable equally spaced, and Valerius appeared, cutting through the crowd with a single felt-clad step that added no sound to his words.

'Question your own sons, Suilius. If you've not seen me before, they have had every proof that I am a man!'

'Will justice, for the first time, balance fate?' muttered the Emperor, becoming interested.

Then he spoke out:

'Stay there, and speak.'

Valerius the Asiatic was of average height, increased by high tight shoes with upturned toes. Vigorous for his age, his baldness was the creation of the razor's polish, but there was a long jet-black plait which fell whip-like and brushed his thighs through a robe of gold-embroidered silk—in the fashion of that country remote from the memory of all men save Amometus.[23] It was to China, whose customs he had adopted without reservations, that Valerius had carried the name of Rome, and he had subsequently bought it as close to Rome as Tartary and India, by importing its silks, furs, slaves and gems to the depots of Dioscurias, where the merchants of seventy peoples converged.

His defence was peremptory (could he have been Poppea's lover when she had been discovered with the mime Mnester in his own gardens? And his great riches, did he use them for aught but the service of the Emperor?) And he so moved Claudius that his trembling seemed caused by emotion. He even drew tears from Messalina.

She left the room to dry her eyes and to command Vitellius the consul ensured the accused did not escape.

Claudius began to speak in Greek, a characteristic sign of great pre-occupation, as often compassionate as sanguinary:

Ετατιλίου δὲ Ταύρου μετὰ Λουκίου Λίξωνος ὑπατσαντος, ὁ Τιξριος ἀπεῖπεν ἐσθῆτι σηρικῇ μηδένα ἄνδρα χρῆσθαι

('Tiberius, under the consulate of Statilius Taurus and Lucius Libon, forbade men from wearing silken robes.')

He appeared to dismiss all charges against the Asiatic save this *promiscuity* of clothing. Silks and stuffs from Cos were reserved for women in the sumptuary laws, (a pound of silk was worth a pound of gold in Rome). Claudius seemed disposed to give him absolution.

Messalina re-entered, preceded by Vitellius.

'That hairy plait upon his head,' she thought, 'is the same as the one that sprouts from between the buttocks of Pan. He protects the god . . . and his nails, they are divine claws!'

'Caesar!' she cried. 'He has his little finger nail in a reed case! You must remember that since that criminal accidently scored your cheek (the scar is its recollection) with his stylus, you wisely forbade even the scribes from carrying their writing-cases in your presence!'

'Am I afraid?' mused Claudius. 'I, a child of the gods?'

'Hear me, Caesar,' said Messalina. 'He keeps the god, the gardens, the globe . . . Caesar! I mean he has the checker-board that Pompey won at his third triumph, made of Sidon glass . . . no, of two different coloured precious stones, four feet long and three feet wide, so massive it bears a gold moon of thirty pounds weight, and with all its pieces sculpted from the same two stones!'

'Venus? . . .' drooled Claudius.

'Lucullus played at being Emperor, and the Asiatic conspires in the same gardens.'

'By the name of Augustus,' said Claudius, painfully, 'Hercules, god of strength, before whose temple I usually pass judgement, Hercules of the Muses, inspire me to a memorable verdict! For I am no arbiter but merely an instrument of Destiny.'

'He mounts his horse on the wrong side,' insinuated Suilius loudly.

26

'He fed his sick father with soup made from human flesh, and celebrated funerals. (I can almost excuse this crime, when I think of his delight at the murder of a Caesar!) He eats with artificial fingers,[24] and observe, he sits instead of standing in your imperial presence, and apparently by Pollux, he imagines he is being duly reverent. He makes love to flies in his bath, and built his library and picture gallery from the roof downwards!'

'Phales starts on Olympus,' thought Messalina aloud.

She caught herself:

'The Asiatic certainly conspires, Caesar!'

Vitellius, who had not yet spoken, now broke the general silence which he had awaited.

'Since his gulit is uncertain, and this aspect of his crime must surely merit some consideration, permit him—for I have always been his friend and I know Caesar's great clemency—permit him to choose the manner of his own death!'

The Asiatic remained perfectly still during thes speeches, in the attitude of a rare, mute and exotic idol, his innocence in a golden robe.

'Ah, my clemency. A great grace certainly!' said Claudius. 'I am very good.' his mouth dripped.

'He is innocent, I think, this man in silk, for the witnesses who claim to have seen his crimes have only identified my secretary. But fate . . . that is real justice. In the name of Augustus and by Hercules, I will allow him to choose the manner of his death! But he must not innovate too much, nor import strange deaths incompatible with the *customs of the ancestors*. Vitellius is your friend, Asiatic, as I now aim to be, by giving you this wise advice: you are young, you can scarcely be more than forty, and therefore have the right to shave your beard with a razor, and leave the tonsure to younger men! But you have already given yourself a bone-white crown with that razor of real Seric steel. You like things that cut then, and preserve the sharpness of your nails with wooden sheaths. Take your bath this evening, and scratch out your life from the base of your neck, Asiatic. It does not lie very deep, a little deeper than the roots of your beard perhaps. I can make myself vomit with ease when required, with the help of a rough tickling feather, the goddess of Fortune. Sleep in a red bath—it is good, better than soft feathers twisted in the ears, I think. I am your good, good friend, Asiatic. I shall be glad to grant the desire that these lying witnesses have attributed to you, and thus make your death a pleasure—you shall dye yourself with all the imperial purple that is sealed in your embroidered chest, and slit the throat of a Caesar!'

Ἄνδρ' ἀπαμύνασθαι ὅτε τις πρότερος προτερος χαλεπήνη[25]

'Am I not a great orator?'

The soldiers removed Valerius; this quotation from Homer at the end of Claudius' speech was his habitual dismissal of those he had condemned to death.

And Messalina cried out in turn, after the silent departure of the Asiatic:

'You are no god then, since you die! But you are content to faint away forever behind the tightly shut doors of your garden (which I shall open), at the feet of the God of the gardens! Just like Lucullus, who died in 'The Apollo',[26] his favourite dining-hall, when he feasted with Phales. For I know that he did not survive the love philter that Callisthenus, his freeman, gave him in order to recover his master's heart, lost to the god! May I be worthy of the table of the god (may the god hear me now), when the time of my apotheosis comes—*Atropus* in the gardens of Lucullus!'

The following evening, when she usually left the palace in disguise for the Suburra, but on this occasion blazing in a great purple cloak beneath which was hidden a lacquer case containing the small bronze key twisted into the form of a dragon that was the key to the garden door; she dismissed the whole company, as a sign that this gift had the finality of a legacy, and forgot to lie to Claudius as to her destination.

He was falling asleep, exhausted by Venus, with no more thought of the sentence he had passed that day, and just comprehended she had said something to do with a door.

'Beware *of the dog,*' the Emperor dreamed.

But Messalina was wholly absorbed in picturing the uncertain vision of a corner of Lucullus' garden, which was the favourite extravagance of the most refined garden architects, after they had exhausted the flowers and sculpture, and all the multi-coloured complexities of horticulture—it was a rough bit of naked field, naked like the nakedness of a man, surrounding a fig-wood ithyphallus. As is customary, the vegetable divinity, crowned with ears of grain, with rocket growing around it, lacked neither of the two attributes that frightened the little children; its vermilion colour, and its keen blade to ward off thieves. The great pinion of its immemorial scythe, one half of Atropus infinite scissors (is the crimson stem of love its twin steel?) *sowed* death all through the field with that *other* gesture that exemplifies the fructifying god.

IV

THE EMPRESS IN PURSUIT OF THE GOD

"Όπου καὶ νῦν ἐπιδοσιν τοιαύτην
τῆς τρυφῆς ἐχούσης οἱ Λουκουλλιανοὶ
κῆποι τῶν βασιλικῶν ἐν τοῖς πολυτε-
λεστάτοις ἀριθμοῦνται
ΠΛΟΥΤΑΡΧΟΥ Λουκούλλου λθ.[27]

It is possible that Poppea, the daughter of Poppeus Sabinus and mother of that Poppea who married Nero, to whom she bequeathed both her beauty and her secret methods for its preservation, was not the mistress of Valerius the Asiatic. Nevertheless Messalina was simultaneously revenged on both the master of the Gardens and her rival in the mirror. What is certain is that the knights known as the Petran, were subsequently accused by Suilius of allowing their palace to be used as a trysting-place by the wife of Cornelius Scipio.

But it was never shown to be the Asiatic whom she met there. The manuscripts of Tacitus which give these meetings as the reason for her execution by the Petran knights do not state 'the trysting-place of Poppea and Valerius', although they are generally so translated (by Lallemand, Brotier, Oberlin, Dureau, de Lamelle, Juste-Lispe, Ernesti, Burnouf). The man's name given in the manuscript is *Nester*, or *Nestor*, or *Vester*. Dotteville conjectures: *Mnester*.

If the rest of this history, and what we know of the actor from Cassius Dio,[28] make a liason between Mnester and a woman seem improbable, one may perhaps presume that the Asiatic paid the actor to provide him with an alibi.

Now, after the Empress had paid Poppea's servants to persuade her to commit suicide in preference to imprisonment; a bizarre, goat-legged form sprang from the house of the Petras, its frantic leaps disguising whether it was clothed or furred, and fled towards the gardens.

That year was marked by several prodigies, near the Isle of the Beast a smaller island emerged from the sea, and Messalina violated the iron lock of Lucullus' park with the little bronze dragon.

The night was piled up more silent and heavier between the high surrounding walls and the first buildings of the villa; and the porter's traditional cerberus, which Claudius had predicted, was a spectre in its pallor.

But it was only a porcelain dog, sitting with a ball under one of its fore-paws, a colossal monochrome vase with glass eyes, its mass perforated and attenuated so that the locks of its long hair seemed to tremble more really in the breeze than the surrounding flower petals.

Past this guardian dog that imitated the fading of a rose, holly-trees were trimmed into animal curves, and gradually as the lawn was flooded by that paler dawn which is the forerunner of moonlight, black silhouettes seemed to battle in the sky with great quadrupedal nephilibates.[29] They faced each other, posed in the shapes of deer, elephants, mantichores or unicorns, disciplined in arabesques of box.

Box shaped into animals was the common adornment of all Roman gardens, but in the garden of the Asiatic keen-eyed architects had carried the art to its limit and beyond, just as his ancestors had crossed those fabled rivers, the Camber and the Lanus, which allowed him to annexe the attributes of Lucullus.

And the box-trees formed their mysterious calligraphies, from top to base, down the promenades.

Here and there, alternating regularily with the finest Greek statues and idols from India and Persia, carved in the richest substances, and Chinese gods with their great bellies, were yews emulating amphora. Then a spiral row of dwarf shrubs, stunted by remorseless pruning, formed the narrowing channel of a labyrinth in whose centre a dry wall of masonry masked off the never-ending shelving box.

But Messalina could not find the sacred fig-trees, rubicund on the acanthus green, that dominated all Roman gardens, dried up yet ripe, smeared with purest Asian vermilion, that sparkled in the sun all day long, and even bespattered the windows of the Caesars!

And neither beneath the ingeniously deformed shrubbery, pruned like a dwarf imprisoned by a leash, nor in the forest of false trees constructed with paper paste or cement—like those that nowadays surround the gardens of inns outside Paris, caricaturing familiar species of tree—could she discover that paroxysm of the garden's beauty, the god's mirror, that ball of Sidon glass!

Unless it were the moon which rose like a lamp held up to help her in her searching.

She deduced that there was no need for idols within the demesne where the god himself walked; no phallic images in the presence of Phales, no mirror, even a marvellous sphere, when the resplendent form itself was imminently manifest.

At the end of the parterre were the valve-like entrances of the dining-halls of Lucullus.

Messalina pushed a door so massive and carefully concealed, she guessed it must guard the obscurest subterranean vault. Inside she was surprised to find a large roofless courtyard bathed in moonlight, quadrangular, the symmetry created by four plane-trees lamenting over the mirror of a central pool of black marble such as is contained in every atrium—their Marsyasian torture.

But this pool of limpid water was an always immaculate cloth on which floated platters shaped like small ships, carrying sweetmeats. Their white emptiness lent them an obscene resemblance to *scaphes*, which are oblong chamber-pots.

Deeper inside, the centre of a plot of earth was bare but for an apple-tree and a tiny pyramid of rockery, another triclinium with beds of jasper was roofed with the artificial verdure of a painted and varnished ivy vine of metal.

Then there was a third retreat, where a window rattled in the breeze of a mechanical wind and the spray of an artificial wind—the cloud was a tall acqueduct. Opposite, a sky-light observed the calmness of the night and the moon sliding up the hillsides of cloud.

Then there was an immense round hall, like Agrippa's Pantheon, which was ventilated by a circular opening in the dome, so high that the interior was entirely sheltered from the wind—and a brief shower, a genuine celestial rain this time, descended vertically into the central pool which was exactly equal in diameter to the opening above, and not a drop inclined toward the dry circumference of pavement.

And then so many doors, with open sky suddenly succeeding crypts, that Messalina no longer knew whether it would be a blank wall or the night air that faced her with its opaque ivory lie.

And when she pushed aside a last vegetable or metallic hanging between the two shafts of an avenue, it joined all its scales hermetically behind her; and there remained no other path towards the outside, save for a stairway leading to another vault.

V

THE FATHER OF THE PHOENIX

*Paullo Fabio, L. Vitellio consulibus, post longum
seculorum anbitum, avis phoenix in Aegyptum venit . . .
Et primam adulto curam sepelcendi patris . . . subire
patrium corpus, inque solis aram perferre atque adolere.*
C. C. TACITI *Annalium lib. VI, 28*[30]

Meanwhile the Asiatic returned to his house, and before all else dictated his last testament in monosyllables to a scribe, who set it down with two brushes on rice-paper in grass-writing, which is almost tachygraphic, and swift as the east wind that lays the grasses before it.

And he said openly that it would have been more honourable to perish by the craft of Tiberius or the violence of Caius Caesar, than by the fraud of a woman and the shameless slander of Vitellius.

Then he rode on horse-back through the precincts within his walls, diverted himself with his daily exercises and dined joyously to the harmonious ringing of cymbals with his concubines, whose feet were so small he thought of them as always lost in the distance, and whose armpits were odorous of tea.

During this meal the gardeners built a pyre, they diligently utilized all the pruned fig-trees with high trunks and no shoots, the precious sculpured masts of cedar and sandal-wood, the great stakes with heads of roots—incorruptible as they had been planted upside down and wood can only rot in the direction of the rising sap.

It was for this reason that Messalina found neither lingam nor ithyphallus silhouetting its tall pale[31] above the thickets of the garden.

Valerius approved the structure of round pillars, already reddened with lacquer like fire, but ordered the pyre be moved elsewhere, for fear of singeing the luxuriant foliage in the burning aura.

He left his stewards to find a treeless space in the park, a simple task for it was so immense even he had never explored it fully.

His final calm recommendation was that, immediately his body was consigned to the flames, the women and slaves should abandon it and trouble the repose of the woods no more; and that the last to leave, making the park a desert, should remove his testament, indecipherable save to his kin—his only explicit codicil concerned the key to his garden gates, which he presented to the Empress.

Then, sitting on his bed, he plunged the razor into the side of his neck, and with his throat stretched taut, gently rocked his naked skull and transparent face from side to side, and death was already visible inside, like a silkworm rising to weave a thread. The tenuous silk of his arterial blood, by this shuttling movement, wove a winding-sheet of purple like a beard over the suddenly senile body and the white cushions.

Then the body, shrouded in asbestos, was carried into the treeless space—bare of trees apart from the dead trunks of the sandal-wood pyre, whose exotic dryads had preceded their master to the bright yellow inferno. The flame clenched its fingers around the sheeted corpse, now like a golden egg, or a cocoon swollen with its larva at the end of a thread, or again, like a mummy asleep in the remotest chamber of its labyrinth. Then it expanded and opened out in a great brilliance, skywards like an exhaled breath, an inhaled breath, the scattered breath, the raised breath, and the reunited breth of all the trees, all the books, all the statues, gems and stuffs, and rose up as if the whole Orient had been imprisoned in the yellow skull and swollen belly of the Asiatic.

And the outspread wings of the Phoenix appeared, which is a real bird since it has been seen in Egypt, the last was born in the reign of Tiberius—the learned describe it as an allegory of the periodic rebirth of the arts in astronomical cycles, whose length they calculate as the period between the bird's burning and rebirth.

Out of their dry sheaths the long nails of flame raised up on a shield, like a birds feathers bristling in courtship, the asbestos sack swollen with emptiness, the dust of bones and the soul—and the dazzling fabulous wings gripped it, and in the traditional manner, bore *the body of his father* toward the eastern sun.

VI

THE PRIAPUS OF THE ROYAL GARDEN

Oriens murrhina mittit. Inveniunlur enim ibi
pluribus locis, nec insignibus maxim Parthici regni: proecipia,
tamen in Carmania. Humorem putant sub terra densari.
C. PLINII SECUNDI *Nat. Historioe lib. XXXVII 8*[32]

The spiral stairway unrolled as though towards some more enclosed and secret chamber, then ended suddenly on the summit of a naked hill; and Messalina, cloaked in purple, emerged like a tongue from a trap-door into the deserted garden.

She was no more surprised by this unforseen change than on those occasions when she passed, fresh from her siesta, through a double door from her sleeping chamber on the Palatine, into the tumult of the Circus Maximus.

The hill was cut (with no barrier for the unwary) by an immense crevasse whose distant circumference could just be distinguished at the very limit of vision, and it appeared to be concave, and would have resembled a crater, had it not been more oval than circular, and in every way similar to an amphitheatre.

It was Lucullus' hippodrome.

And just as the modern purchaser of a tiny suburban garden, careworn and distracted, might allow the ornamental fish pond to dry up, so the Asiatic had paid no attention to this great black lake behind the thickets, and with a similar negligence he had allowed the luxuriant grasses to achieve their ultimate tangled flourishes. And he had abandoned the arena—as distant in the depths of the circus as if it were built to seat a hundred thousand—to the whims of his gardeners.

Three and four-horse ploughs had re-etched the furrows for season after season before they had eventually removed the ancient crystal sand and mixed it with the black earth of their tracks. And, following Homer's teaching as represented on Achille's shield, after every turn of the parallel tracks around the two porphry pillars topped with eggs of gold, the aurigan[33] ploughman emptied a large cup into the great cup of the circus

And like the dances of women and goddesses engraved in niello about the tops of cups and craters, Messalina sought a less vertiginous descent, and raced around the border of the highest tier of the gigantic stairway. As the eye penetrated further into the abyss each successive circular stair constituted a yet smaller crown —the last circled the prostrate brow of the night, and was too remote for the Empress to discern whether it fitted as exactly as her courtesans wig.

The moon was full, but no longer showed its face in the sky, and it was through white clouds swollen with moon-milk that the masked light flowed over the far margin of the amphitheatre, tinting it with the colour of ivory or bone.

Messalina understood with a growing certainty that she must descend, and that the most precious part of the gardens could be nowhere else but here, where the centripetal stairway converged toward the mysterious depths of the Asiatic's pyre—the temple of the god, no doubt!

And ONE FACT pointed her way more imperiously, and then obstructed it momentarily with the resplendent horror of a mystery.

Taking every position in the amphitheatre—which would have seated a hundred thousand—motionless like fascinated undistractable spectators, on the seats of the people, the soldiers, the knights, the magistrates, and the vestals, according to the heirarchy of orders, were *murrhines,* fixed in contemplation of the dark arena beneath.

Murrhines, according to Pliny, are a humour produced by heating earth, just as crystal is produced when it is frozen.

They are precious stones from the Orient (the finest are from Carmania), and cups and platters are carved out of them.

In colour they are purple or an opaque white—veins of blood and milk writhe in their fiery interior.

They are perfumed, and a crack will often provoke moles and warts on their surface, like human skin.

Propertius (IV, v. 26) speaks of 'murrhine goblets baked in Partian hearths', which would suggest a fired sandstone or glass mixture, or according to a modern hypothesis, a sort of chinese porcelain. But, it is known that the substance of murrhines is the work of the earth alone and not of men; they are cups hollowed in a stone that resembles agate, which we would call nowadays fluorate of chalk or fluoride of calcium.

They are among the most prized of gems, for the single murrhine from which Claudius drank had cost the Emperor three hundred talents, or one million four hundred and seventy thousand gold francs.

And forgotten by the Asiatic, powdered with dust and dried manure and bearded with the spider-webs of scattered petals, they blossomed there; for Lucullus had built this enormous hippodrome just to display his murrhines, an ostentation which Nero imperfectly duplicated with the small trans-Tiberian theatre he built for his children.

Their stains of flame disappeared in the light like the stars of star sapphires, and were now motionless. Their squat forms, several as large as small tables, were each balanced on a golden base, like a çompany of cyclopean birds each perched on one foot.

Their fires were tireless covetous eyes or thirsty mouths directed toward the silent spectacle where the black night played the part of choir.

Then Messalina, recovering from her amazement, leapt forward in a fierce race down the steps through the priceless treasures, her cloak billowing and catching in the golden claws and overturning these beasts that were gems. Those that rolled accompanied her, step by step, sighing with joy as they cracked and because they would present themselves to the god, like the Empress, in a female aspect.

At the base her way was blocked by the *podium*—a hedge of junipers from the banks of the Amor and Psitara, covered in blue marguerites (the original colour of these Seric flowers). It covered the arena with a perfectly flat surface, it was taller than a man, stiffer than wheat stubble and was cut by regular paths in the shape of a star. Messalina's gaze was guided toward the centre; here her feet were effortlessly upheld by the elastic petioles for it was carpeted with innumerable tulips and an infinity of amaranths that imitated the murrhines, the former in their shape, the latter in their immortality.

In the centre of the arena, or rather at one of the centres of the ellipse, something resembling an enormous egg vibrated imperceptibly, whiter than the moonlit clouds. Messalina made out a head among the flowers, its nape resting on a cushion of blond hair; two hands were passed between the thighs and curled around the hairy buttocks, and two feet smaller than goats hooves were crossed behind the neck.

Messalina's eyes shone triumphantly. But defying her stare, from the summit of the basket-shaped hill of green porphry to her very feet, were the fiery stars of murrhines, some cracked and gaping here and there on the sward of blue marguerites, immortelles and tulips, others in tiers, like mushrooms whose caps had been turned inside out by a great blast from the depths or by an overwhelming ache to blossom and grow—they opened covetous eyes and thirsty mouths.

She looked at the murrhine of the royal box.

And now the shadow of the edge of the low, wide, gnawed crater (heir of the master's teeth as wax is the widow of the seal) was projected from the height of the imperial box; the width of the hollow bite was amplified and its ragged profile crowned the dwarf with battlements and then devoured him, this confused silhouette—a white ball engrossed in a Narcissistic kiss.

It was the bite of the naked man coiled among the flowers that was the more intense, but Messalina interrupted him. She passed her hand across his downy back which felt like the breast feathers of a nocturnal bird. He unfolded his chest—a rosy stain had been imprinted on it by his mouth and chin —his belly and his Pan's legs. He stretched out his whole figure, the feet joined in the air, the arms and head still on their pedestal of flowers. Then his feet slowly descended back behind his head and all his joints cracked for a second time, but more softly, and now he was upright and standing naturally. Petals of marguerites rained from his disordered hair and from his short clipped beard.

The Empress recognised the face of the god—it was Mnester, a familiar of Caligula, and a celebrated actor whom she had applauded at the Circus.

According to popular rumour he was Poppea's lover, not the Asiatic.

But she continued to believe she was in the presence of the god.

She was pleased that the god loved his own body more than Poppea's.

The god took a few halting steps, staggering just as an ordinary man would were he to imitate Mnester and stand on his head, or perhaps as did the gods when they first set foot on solid earth. Messalina raised her hands, not from curiosity or desire, but to protect herself from the falling body.

And as Priapus himself, or an acrobatic juggler, would finally tire of holding a great tree in equilibrium,—the sex of the god fell in to her hands.

It was so brutal, heavy, and so dreadfully the real presence of Phales, that Messalina fled over the field of blue petals caught at by the flowers, while Mnester, his long body undulating with the serpentine movements of a lamprey—that leech monstrous enough to be beautiful and paler than ivory —went off slowly, like a demiurge rolling a world, to crouch in the temple of new amaranths close by.

And Messalina did not see him again until the Circus.

To the Empress it was as arduous a task to climb the steps of the murrhine-lit hippodrome before dawn as to climb a firmament studded with red-hot nails.

She wandered; and crossed a flowerless, treeless space which was the other centre of the elliptical arena—*it had been its second heart:* for a small thing cracked under her heel with a sound infinitely less perceptible than the cracking of murrhines. A little thing, as she picked it up a thin shadow of dust obscured it. She did not know if it was a poppy's skull or that ivory capsule which the pyre had carved into a rare fragility with greater skill than any sculptor's chisel: the head of the Master of the Trees.

VII

HE DANCED SOMETIMES AT NIGHT

Saltabat autem nonnunquam etiam noctu.
C. SUETONII TRANQUILLI *C. Caligulae LIV*[34]

On the first day of the following calends in August, at the festival celebrating the fifty-eighth anniversary of Claudius' birth, Mnester appeared in Caligula's theatre, or more precisely, on a platform at the foot of Caius' pink granite obelisk carved by Nuncoreus, son of Sesoses; in the centre of Caius' circus at Vaticanus, later re-named the Circus of Nero—and the sound of flutes, the hydraulus and the whistling scabella at last broke the silence of the flowers.

He was clothed in a net of crescent-shaped gold scales each with a projection between the two horns, like hooks covering his flesh, or the marks of love-bites. A larger half-moon of gold hung from his left ear, as though his hairdresser had scorched a lock of his hair. Another on his forehead outlined a pair of frowning eyebrows, and a much larger one served as a *subligar*, or apron, and played the role of a mask imitating the face it conceals.

Like the clanking of a heavier coat of mail, or the booming undertow that accompanies the breaking of the ocean surf, the applause erupted about the sharp steps of his entrance, from the lowest to the highest of the three-tiered sections; from the senator's benches to the immense crowd of commoners; and it filled the circus to the brim.

The people no longer needed to remember the times when, if anyone applauded Caius' favourite with too little enthusiasm, he was dragged by the imperial guards to the pulvinar and the Emperor's right hand would prolong the clapping on the man's cheek, with his left hand hanging motionless at his side.

For this and other reasons—and we can never know if Mnester had real genius—the Roman people never missed his mime.

In the height of the imperial box, Claudius' head twitched nervously and his hands fluttered together in such agitation that a die was ejected from the ivory box fastened to a ring around his middle finger. The uproar was drowned by the sound of Messalina smacking her lips.

Mnester replied with one small smile, his lips red to the point of blackness, were outlined, for some reason, with a rose-coloured tide-line dying or nascent around them, like the penumbra ringing a shadow.

He had been anounced that day as the *exodiarius,* the solo actor in the licentious piece traditionally performed during the interval or after a tragedy instead of an Atellan farce. And the circus gaped in suspense, for the laviscous and clownish dance created by the mime was to depict the tormented spasms of that most horrifically tragic hero—Orestes among the Furies.

The last fragments of applause skipped from place to place, the interrupting pauses became longer until the silence was complete; and simultaneously the surface of Mnester's clinking tunic regained its equilibrium. But, in the midst of increasing amazement, he remained motionless, leaning against, and blending with, the gilded decoration on the base of Caius' pink obelisk, for so long that the ternary rhythym of the flutes and the moist roaring of the hydraulus' eopiles, which were to prelude his dance, faded into expectation just as the clapping hands had done before.

But the people were impatient with that which they did not understand and a new rumbling arose in the circus' throat, one of dissatisfied murmurings, then shouts and insults.

The rose-tinted obelisk pierced the noise implacably, the golden figure against its plinth.

The whistles and jeers broke against this lighthouse (whose light was at its base), harmonized and took on a form which bounded in a reverberating onslaught around the arena:

'Dance, Mnester.'

Then Mnester came forward to the edge of the dias with the weary gesture of one asleep in the sun and disturbed by the buzzing of flies, and said:

'I am sorry, but I cannot, *I have just slept with Orestes.* '35

And he stretched himself out once more on his vertical bed.

In a half silence of whisperings, the physicians and philosophers, and Claudius, considered that the mime's statement ingeniously expressed the exhaustion entailed in creating a great dramatic character; but the people, and Messalina, were too angry for subtleties. The crowd jumped to its feet, shouting insults and gesticulating at Caesar, they pointed at the *Orestes* which rumour and gossip had already accused and sentenced: Messalina, abductress of street-porters, actors and gladiators, who confronted their clamourous maledictions with the cold shield of her stare, impudent and immodest.

'Gentlemen,' stammered Claudius (it was his custom to address the Roman people with this honorific), 'it's not my fault, I have no dealings with him, I too want him to dance, gentlemen.'

'Dance, Mnester,' replied the crowd, redirecting the injunction of their desires at the mime.

'Orestes is all these people, I realise, Mnester, but dance, dance anything, I beseech you, just for me,' cooed Messalina.

'It pleases my wife, the people and myself that I order you to dance,' said Claudius.

'I dance,' said Mnester slowly, 'Caesar and wife of Caesar, for fear of a thousand whiplashes one of which would be a lovebite.'

And so to celebrate the fifty-eighth anniversary of the birth of Claudius, in the theatre of Caligula or rather on a platform at the foot of Caius' pink granite obelisk, in the centre of Caius' circus, to the sound of flutes, the hydraulus and the whistling scabella, Mnester danced.

The tunic of golden scales trembled in the sun like the wind ruffling the back of a river.

All the parts of his supple body seemed to be juggling, each with one another, and each one was followed lovingly in its course by a fragment of sun.

And for the first time—since pantomimes began in the reign of Augustus to illustrate and demonstrate a poem sung by a choir or a soloist— the mime himself sang, as though it were the muffled rustlings of his dancers ornaments.

A muffled rustling: his voice seemed less a voice, so deep is it, than the fluting of his scabella, those hollow dancers sandals, which at each bound, expel air in a single note; or the moaning of the earth's entrails responding to the vibrations of the *many-headed instrument;* the circus's hydraulic organ, invented by the goddess Pallas, constructed in the form of an altar by Pindar Ctesibus of Alexandria, described by Pindar the poet, Hero, Claudian and Vitruvius; *imitated,* according to Cornelius Severus, *by* Etna, and upon which Nero himself vowed to play on the day his life was imperiled.

The mime sang:

In the centre of your circus, Cai, I dance
I dance in the sun,
In an equal splendour
Oh my lovely painted idol, you appeared in a chariot filled with thunder,
And your mouth drank the lightning
Of the golden beard of the red-headed charioteer.

Only you could have drifted in purple silk over the bridge which made

40

dry land of the ocean,
>*At Baulis.*

Illuminating the depths with your Chlamys of precious stones from India.

>*Thousands of men pressed forward to see you*
>*And were immersed in your reflection*
>*Their death was a libation, filling the cup*
>*Of the place of cliffs like a crescent moon.*

>*You won a great victory*
>*On the sands by the sea; against countless legions*
>*For a great victory about five hundred motionless enemies suffice;*
>*And you assumed the toga and palm-wreath legitimately*
>*And you had every right to erect a twelve-storey tower to your memory*
>*At Boulogne,*
>*For you had all the seashells on the shore taken prisoner*
>*By your tall Gauls with red-dyed hair like Germans,*
>*Your beautiful Gauls of triumphal stature.*

>*You pursued with righteous anger*
>*The Jews of Alexandria*
>*Who preferred to you their nameless God*
>*Yet God has a name*
>*He is called* CAIUS[36]

Ah, like your hand on the cheek of he who has not applauded my dance,

Your mouth on my mouth during the spectacle that will interrupt my dance!

'He is speaking of Caius,' grumbled Claudius. 'I can no longer recall whether I forbade the mention of this dead man's memory . . . Yes: I opposed the Senate, who wanted to brand him with infamy . . . but I spent the night toppling his statues!'

'It's Apollo and it is Orpheus,' cried the voices of the crowd. 'If the wild beasts were released into the circus, they'd just lie down . . .'

'People, lie down!' cried Messalina.

And still Mnester bent and dislocated his body, and the *noise* of his deep voice was like the rumbling of cogs engaging, unique and terrible. And

each part of his body, wherever it wandered, was followed lovingly and faith-
fully by a fragment of the sun.

He juggled with the sun's debris.

Claudius, who doted on skilful mimes—he would even sometimes be
left dreaming before the empty stage long after the people had left for their
evening meal—had now forgotten all the others, even Publius the Syrenian. He
leant over the edge of the pulvinar to applaud, and the hot afternoon light
picked out his long neck which was trembling slightly as usual, like quivering
vegetation in the dog days, or like those dolls which, since the time of
Hercules, had superseded the human skulls strung up in honour of Saturn on
the hill devoted to him—the Capitoline.

'It's Orpheus, by Augustus!' exclaimed Claudius, with the people. 'And
it's Amphion,[37] and a Thebes shall be built about the lyre of his body and
the seven planets will descend and enter him through his seven doors!'

The song was no longer intelligible as it crept across the bare ground,
lower than a wild animal's death rattle: for the mime, after a perilous *one
and a half somersaults,* had landed on his hands, posed like a cube, and the
golden scales, now reversed, opened their leaves; the polished half-moons
reflected only shadow; light caressed Mnesters naked body through the
mail's mesh, and his subligar turned down as one might raise a visor.

His murmur became a song once more, distinct as the sounds of the
scabella died away:

In the centre of your circus, Cai, I dance with the sun,
Just as, beloved dead one, BENEATH MY FEET, UP THERE
Someone is playing knuckle-bones with your remains.

The mime made great somersaults on one arm without interrupting or
faltering in his low constant drone; and now he spun faster and faster on his
hand, outspread on the ground, which shone white in the shadow of his
vertical body, like a fallen star.

It seemed impossible that a man could so contort his bones without
them breaking.

Or that he could so shatter the sun, casting it into countless dozens of
tiny mirrors, and yet not finally destroy it totally, with no possibility of
re-assembling it.

Like the growing throb of a brass top, the voice grew loud and great:

At the foot of your sex, Cai
I will dance as Caius danced!

He danced with me in the Circus, in his Circus, in the sun,
With me and the sun,
And also
He danced sometimes at night.

Caius, golden, jewelled idol,
Caius, the moon's lover
Caius, paler from love-making than the pale star
He danced sometimes at night
He had all the torches extinguished, and he himself, since only he
could, he himself...

Mnester no longer sang but was talking to himself in an attitude of meditation, his arms crossed and his head fallen on his chest, he revolved slowly now on the nape of his neck, as if he had done so throughout eternity, like the inert orbits of the stars beneath his joined feet.

... He took the stars from the sky, so supple he could reach the stars in the sky, *he extinguished the sky's torches,* LIKE THIS ... and then ...
HE DANCED ... SOMETIMES ...

And at that moment the dance was invisible.

The Circus was filled with a sudden night, with tumult and horror.

A black disk bit into the very substance of the sun, until only a red crescent remained like the *penumbra* of Mnester's lips and the thousands of suddenly purple crescents of his tunic's mesh devoured his sidereal flesh with the fathomless gluttony of mirrors. The luminary was charred like the expiration of a smoking lamp.

'This is Caesar's birthday! Only an ill-omened Caesar can cause such prodigies! It was he forced the mime to dance! Death to Caesar! Death to his whore! Caius has returned from the underworld!'

These and a thousand other cries struggled, after a long moment of stupor, to escape the folds of the appalling darkness.

The music had been snuffed out with the sun, save for one flute-player who had suddenly gone quite mad, and was blowing the same shrill note continuously as long as his breath held: and the prodigous trumpet of the steam-organ floundered like a panicked elephant, and stamped out its automatic, joyous and unbearable triple rhythm.

Over the top edge of the Circus, just above the pulvinar, a last red ray flickered, picking out the habitual tottering of Claudius' head, as if he were

43

holding up this supreme piece of flotsam to the furious despairing gaze of the ship-wrecked mob.

The spectators had no more thought of the mime as the curtain of the night unfurled.

In the last imperial light only Messalina's eyes, blacker than two extinguished coals, were fixed on the indestructible shadow in the base of the Circus—where Mnester's last, most silent, action reached its finale.

'Gentlemen,' began the stammering Claudius, and all his teeth (some were false) chattered like thirty-two die in a bleeding dice-box, but his paroxysms of fear and trembling increased and jumbled his syllables. He stopped stammering and, standing upright, held up his hand to the crowd, his hair a bright crown in the last blood-light of the sun.

In a single breath, he shouted:

'Gentlemen, listen. It is I, Caesar, Emperor, god and augur, versed in all the mathematical sciences, even music and astronomy. It is I that speaks. THIS IS AN ECLIPSE![38] The moon, gentlemen, which as you know rotates beneath the sun, either immediately below or with Mercury and Venus between, and is moving in the same latitude as this star . . . Did none of your sons, noble senators, return from Etruria suitably instructed in our ancient and sacred doctrines of Haruspicy, are they unable to decipher the entrails of the sky as well as those of the sacrifices? There is no danger! The mime is no astrologer! . . The moon is moving longitudinally . . . Keep back, but listen! And, besides, Agrippa expelled the Chaldeans and astrologers from the City! But the moon, you'll recall, also moves latitudinally, unlike the sun! . . and so it passes before the sun obscuring it with its shadow! During the questorship of Drusus, my father, Augustus forbade astrologers to predict a person's death! Resume your seats! The eclipse should last a quarter of an hour, there is no need even to light the torches! The moon will remove the sun's blindfold.

Claudius fell back on the cushions of his box, losing his scarlet aura and wiping the foam from his mouth with Messalina's handkerchief.

The sun resumed its place and the crowd returned its gaze to the sphingitic arena, to reassure themselves that it was no longer too red.

But when the spectators looked at each other, having stared so fixedly at the reappearing star, in place of each head they saw only a black stain and the whole circus seemed peopled with negroes.

Something had rolled over the edge of the stage where it continued to occult the light, casting a shadow on the ground. It was a ball as perfectly round as the disk of a fallen planet, the inextricably *curled-up* body of Mnester at the end of his dance. Now, a curled-up body is an astronomical

44

term—*'glomeramen'*,[39] signifying the libation of the moon—as Vectius Valens pedantically observed when, on Messalina's orders the mime was carefully carried to the palace of the Caesars, to the clamour of the rejoicing crowd, content again, and to the sounds of the flute and hydraulus.

And Messalina that evening in bed, fifty-eight years exactly since the birth of Claudius, whispered, 'Claudii, husband, emperor, god,' she repulsed him as she did when insisting on some trivial and paradoxical caprice, 'Caesar, augur, versed in music, even astronomy: *I want* THE MOON.'

THE LEGITIMATE ADULTERIES

I

BENEATH DIANA PERSIA'S LAMP

Siquidem Latinarum feriis quadrigae
certant in Capitolio, Victorique absinthium bibit.
C. PLINII SECUNDI *Nat. Historiae* lib.XXVII, 28.[40]

H e is no longer unconscious, but he remains motionless, and does not speak,' reported the physician, returning to the grotto.

This cavern was the coolest triclinium of Lucullus' summer house, the subterranean and submarine hall of Anaitis, Diana Persia, cooler still than the cavernous house which was Tiberius' country residence at Terracina, out of which he made the imperceptible transition to the iciness of steel, then death. Over the walls were stretched whole tanned hides of Euphrates cows, and set in their flanks, instead of sacred lamps, were gleaming panes of glass, bright with light reflected through the salt waters of the Tiber which roared behind the walls—all constructed by Lucullus, an architect so skilled in the building of acqueducts he had been acclaimed as the Roman Xerxes.

'The god clasps his fist over the enigmas of his heart even more tightly than in his temple of porphry and immortelles,' pondered Messalina. 'Claudius,' she said, 'the mime, Mnester, refuses to obey me in one thing.'

Claudius did not at first reply, his ear to the grinding through the crystal windows. Outside, flasks of wine, so ancient and encrusted with coral they looked like the distended and disembowelled bodies of animals, lay among the debris of crab-claws and ventral fins—a refuse in a continuous vertiginous agitation from the king-crabs whose backs sealed the bottle-necks and preserved their contents. Then the glass echoed to the boom of a Taprobanian drum, and a diver descended with a stone gripped between his thighs to retrieve oysters from Burdigala, the sorcerer's music protecting him for the duration of his inhaled breath from the vigilance of the guardian shark of the circular moat.[41]

'What thing?' said Claudius.

But Messalina's thoughts held their breath with the diver, and the cup-bearer, a soldier, took this opportunity to drop a new fragment of Falerno in the Emperor's cup of hot water.

Claudius drank, and his cheek purpled, heightening the pallor of the cicatrice, the wound made by a stylus:

'It was I who renewed the custom, which had fallen into disuse, of choosing actors from among the slaves! And Augustus, though restricting the punishments of slaves, upheld them for histrions! So, the mime must obey you, Valeria, in all things!'[42]

A more formidable clanging prolonged the quavering of Claudius' order. Tanned hides constituted the skin of the room from the windows up to the vaulted ceiling—the remainder was lined with casques and faces, eyes duller than the jade pupils of cows—the lightning of the soldiers' javelins was packed tight along the walls.

For since the first, imaginary, attempts on his life, the Emperor never *reclined* for a repast unless the army were a part of the dinner service.

On an order from the Empress, with Claudius' consent, a lictor went out to Mnester. He returned, much later, with his switches bloody and broken.

'He does not speak, he crumpled up and rolled on the floor,' the lictor said.

'Now he is adorned with a trellis of little crescents of blood, as when he eclipsed the sun, both times in the Circus,' said Messalina.

And her tongue made a thousand and first red lunula in her memory.

'He just refuses to,' said Vectius Valens, who was drinking on the third bed, opposite the Emperor.

'And yet you claim to have selected him from among your slaves,' she cried.

But Claudius had fallen asleep, his cheek slashed by his elbow. And on his little table of Arbor Vitae his only response was to shake and upset his great cup, scarlet clots rolled out and stained the three beds and the path between them that was left clear for the slaves.

Messalina turned on her couch towards the physician:

'Perhaps a philtre would be more efficacious than whips and blood to make one love who only loves himself, like Artemis the virgin, who turns her back on the heavens and inclines one crescent towards the other? I am certain now it is a god that possesses me, and not merely an actor slave I have had beaten. Can you conjure up the gods, physician?'

'Artemis, you said?' said Valens, scarcely interrupting his drinking. '*Artemesia*, absinthe, is itself a philtre.[43] Artemis, Luna, Phoebe, triple Hecate! There are three types of absinthe: the first is Gallic, or *santonic*, with golden hair. *Pontic*, the second, is from the distant Orient where they fatten cattle on it so they are sometimes found to have no gall so, just as we can see the light from the river through the livers of these cows, flayed like the foeti the high vestal burns during the festival of Palilas, Valeria, pontic is the best; but the third, the absinthe of Italy is more bitter . . .

'I do not require a hippomane for a bull, but for Priapus the god!' said

Messalina.

'You can dissolve artemisia a day and a night in salt rainwater, and you will have that same absinthe a cup of which, in our ancient Latin festivals, was the highest prize for the quadriga race at the foot of the Captol, the prize that stood above the crown of gold! For in water it gives sovereign health and clarifies the sight, although in wine, to tell the truth, it is an antidote to the venoms of hemlock, the sea-dragon, the shrew-mouse and the scorpion! Inhaled it provokes sleep, and will be perfectly efficacious if slipped beneath Mnester's pillow without his knowledge!'

The Empress, hardly able to remember any of these formulae, fled the presence of the loquacious physician.

I shall write down for you the remaining properties of absinthe,' he hiccoughed through Claudius' snores, 'ink made of absinthe [44] is safe for posterity as it is secure from rats!'

For a day and a night it rained a warm melting rain like tears of joy, and Messalina had gathered the plant from which the philtre was to be made; Vectius asked:

'Has he drunk?'

'He has drunk,' replied Messalina, radiant and furious with a new form of voluptuousness and renewed anger. 'He has drunk, tractably, until he is no longer Phales, nor Mnester, but like a tiny baby in his cradle, who has forgotten himself—and me!'

'Absinthe infused a day and a night in rain-water is, in fact, an emmenagogue for women, but for men constitutes a diuretic,' pronounced the physician Vectius Valens gravely.

Now the populace were not long in complaining outside the palace of the Caesars when they discovered this theft of their mime. And Messalina, as if throwing handfuls of gold into the heart of a riot, had many statues of Mnester cast out of Caius' bronze money, which the senate had approved, and they were raised throughout the Empire.

And these effigies, like golden eggs, perpetuated the Narcissistic gesture of the gardens, and the heavenly body of Caius' theatre.

Modern excavations have uncovered one of these statues in the piscine at Capri.

Vectius Valens examined the metal portraits with interest:

'So this is Phales?'

'Oh yes,' said Messalina, 'it was a very little child, but it was certainly presence of Phales. Phales, Priapus, the god of love, is a modest little child who hides himself behind a tree which he carries everywhere.'

'And for a more secret refuge, he finds the women with the tenderest sap-wood,' Vectius jested.

'It was really Priapus. I saw him,' repeated Messalina, obstinately.

'For us hereafter, according to the most indisputable ocular testimony,' the physician concluded, 'Priapus is a frigid man.'

II

THE MOST BEAUTIFUL OF THE ROMANS

C. Silium, juventutis romanae pulcherrimum.
C. CORNELII TACITI *Annalium* lib. XI, 12.[45]

It was no doubt from having created numerous representations of Mnester that Messalina one day realized that they had but a single model; and it was not in her character to hesitate long between a single god, even one of love, and a plural number of men.

She conceived an ardent passion for a young patrician, C. Silius Silanus, consul-designate, who during the trial of the knights of Petras, following Poppea's death, had moved her with his fluent exaltation of the ancient honour of the orators (which was greatly in vogue at that time among orators in public places) and especially of Corvinus Messalla, Messalina's ancestor, and with his stigmatizing of Suilius the informer, whom she had made her own only by recalling him from an island exile.

He also dazzled her with his vermilion complexion, his jet-black beard, the grand gestures of his heavy hands, whose little finger dilated a golden ring, and with his protrusive lips like an extra tongue.

The Empress and her great company of former lovers—the freedmen (save the lictor Polybus, whose death she had arranged following a lovers quarrel), Callistus, who pretended to have saved Claudius from poisoning during Caius' reign, Narcissus, Evodus, Pallas, descendant of the kings of Arcady, a noble slave, Caesar's attendant, and Vectius Valens the physician—were now selling the rights of citizenship 'like tavern-keepers', Dio reports,[46] even to Bretons, and also any other privileges they could dispose of; so that in a short time, but not as fast as the palpitations of her heart, Messalina felt the jewelled purse swelling, fastened ostentatiously over her left breast.

Meanwhile Claudius, ignorant of these events, ordered the execution of all those who seemed to him to be usurping the title of citizen, and Messalina and Pallas re-sold each title to the highest bidder, as it was vacated.

Messalina collected great quantities of gold, for experience had taught her that a rich and noble lover, a consular personage of well-known integrity, was distinguished by one fact—that he must be bought nobly dear.

Now Silius was not only a consular personage, honourable and wealthy, but he was recently married and made a great show of his love for his young wife Junia.

In consequence, numerous presents were laid at the feet of this new god and when the gold was exhausted, it was followed by all the riches of the Neros and the Drusi that had been amassed in the palace of the Caesars, even Pompey's chequer-board. Claudius' fixed and bovine eye saw nothing, due to the ever-increasing trembling of his face. Even the Emperor's own slaves were dispatched, each one of which was called *Christ* or *Chrest*, a certificate of their great value ; as was the single gold statue of Mnester.

On the day the last treasure (save the imperial bed)—the portrait of Messalina in pearls, was taken down from the Palatine on the shoulders of the remaining female slaves; only then, behind the last slave, did the Empress offer herself to Caius Silius.

Silius found her imperial and beautiful, and he particularily remembered the death of Appius Silanus, Messalina's father-in-law, whose head was cut off for conspiracy. For surely it must be conspiracy to refuse the desires of *the Augusta*? And there was also the poisoning of Vicinius Quartinus, consul, and many other deaths.

Imperial.

And, as one may fall in love by contagion with a beautiful woman in love, the eloquent consular personage, whom the City had unanimously proclaimed the most beautiful of all Romans, felt the passion of the Empress envelope him and tighten its circles until it bound his temples with an Emperor's crown.

For this reason, and for her beauty, he loved her.

Messalina had come altogether naked, like a slave displayed to her purchaser; she was covered, while awaiting the master's possessive arms, in the great cloak that concealed the courtesan of the Suburra, or the pursuer of the God of the Gardens.

The stuff that caressed her body was the mantle of the Suburra, for the golden wig was superflous in making her a courtesan.

And now, before her actual lover, as at the feet of Phales, or in the street of prostitutes—which is the wake of love traced by his passage—it seemed as if the Night itself, a shivering bird, was sheltering in the heart of the folds of shadow.

For this divinity of darkness a ray of sunshine was as a freezing rain in comparison to the voluptuous incense of a just-extinguished lamp in the lupanar.

But it was not (as a detail revealed) the garment of the night in the lupanar, but of the evening in the Asiatic's hippodrome, which Messalina removed in Silius' house!

But it is a logical and human failing to be misled by this external appearance, and so Claudius absurdly *wagered* that she belonged to him alone, on the very days she returned home reeking of Lycisca's smoky cell!

That night in the Asiatic's arena, a tiny murrhine, as though fallen from its nest, had clamped itself to her train with the whole strength of its broken claws; and as she had not worn the cloak since, she only noticed the pink milk-spattered stone long after she had cast aside the mantle, like a mellower carpet, on the fur-covered flagstones of Silius' cubiculum.

She offered him this last gem—his lovers mouth had already gathered the gold from her breasts—and when the couple rested on his bed, a young boy was called to pour foaming Cecuba into the wonderful jewel and cup.

Then the most beautiful of the Romans, on his belly, raised himself on both elbows, and knit his brows at Messalina's hand, tendering him the cup. The Empress had dragged it down the steps in her rrush to the arena, and plain between her outspread fingers the crack wept—a clepsydra counting off the hours of love.

Disdainfully, after all this homage paid him in the form of perfect treasures, his malicious look implied the giver was no longer flawless, like this latest gift.

'Are you not jealous, Valeria, to give me all these female things?'

'My sex is the lesser,' she replied, with a gesture.

III

THE ADULTEROUS NUPTIALS

Οὐδέ τι οἶδα
Εἰ μοι ἔτ' ἔμπεδόν ἐστι, γύναι, λέχος —
ΟΔΥΣΣΕΙΑΣ Ψ. [47]

The bed of the Caesars had not been carried off to Silius' house like the furniture, the slaves and Messalina's love, but the reason was not that it was rooted to the floor of the palace like Ulysses' Homeric couch nor because it is more natural for a man to walk to a bed than a bed to a man, but because in Messalina's mind the bed of the Caesars required as its canopy the whole palace of the Caesars, from its foundations—the deepest being Rome itself, to its pinnacle—the Emperor, Claudius Caesar (who, at this moment was writing his history of Rome in the transparent belvedere, and his plodding erudition had yet to perceive the sudden catastrophe that was occuring in his narrative).

But there came a dawn when the wide nuptial couch—its squat ivory feet circled with silver, with panels entirely of the same virgin metal, after the fashion of Delos, and covered with purple, embroidered with eagles—bowed silently under the naked and muscular weight of Silius, whose black beard made the white silk of the sheet, and Messalina's shoulder, appear yet more dazzling.

The close-shaved face of Claudius had lately tinted everything in this room the colour of grey hair.

This did not oppress the Emperor, being a slight rejuvenation, though without any prospect of a return to a pre-imperial adolescence.

Before he had grey hair he had not been Venus' lover.

Pale locks, they plaited the dawn of his imperial crown.

As for the greatest whiteness of all, Claudius did not confront it directly, and the shaking of his head could no doubt be compared to a cornered swan stretching its neck to right and left, where there is no hunter, for life is not a long enough inhalation of breath for its song of apotheosis.

And as Silius stretched himself out on his bed, scarcely in Messalina's arms, he showed a sudden anguish, as he had at the sight of the goblet, so real that Messalina forgave him at once, and even repented the fault she imagined she must have unknowingly committed.

Silius searched, fumbled feverishly with both hands, under the vast nakedness of his shoulders, and captured what it was that was causing his discomfort—had an insect bitten him?

Livid, angular, crystalline, sharp, senile, obscene, naked to the bone. A die.

'You should have kept one slave at least,' said Silius, standing on the carpet, 'to change Caesar's sheets.'

'But I have given you everything Silius,' sobbed Messalina. 'I didn't think you would pay any attention . . . to that thing. I didn't think you would even find it. Claudius' sheets were left on the bed as innocently as if he had been dispatched from this bed at your entrance in heroic costume . . . I should have loved it on his body . . .'

(In heroic costume, that is to say altogether naked, but for some drapery over the left shoulder.)

'. . . But I have given you my whole life! I love you, Silius! My body, which you do not reject . . . will you also peel off my skin which belongs to Claudius? I love you!'

'Yes, Valeria, you love both of us well enough—I am not counting the herd of others—both of us, *me and Caesar.*'

'Get up! You have given me nothing, not even a part of your love, since Caesar's portion is no smaller for the gift! Or, if you have given me all . . . who absolutely possesses Caesar's wife is . . . Caesar! I am your legitimate husband, perhaps it is only through fear of repudiating my ancestral Caesars that I, like them, have not chastised he who has for all these years been so fearfully adulterous in my own palace. He has left me my wife only now, this night, the first . . . that is why I am unable to repudiate her; we have not yet enjoyed our nuptial night, for me, until tonight . . . *(Silius wept)* MESSALINA IS VIRGIN!'[48]

'You are right, ab-so-lutely right, Silius,' said Messalina.

'Silius! Why yes: Silius! I am going mad!' said Silius. 'Everything I have said is absurd. I have stolen the treasures of the Caesars and robbed Caesar of his wife, *like everyone else*, that is all. I am nothing but Silius, consul-designate, a private citizen, husband of Junia Silvana. Ha ha ha! Husband of the Augusta! So where is our marriage contract, Empress? The legal proof?'

'You are Caesar absolutely, O Caesar!' said Messalina, on her knees.

IV

THE IMITATION OF BACCHUS

Καὶ σύμπασιν ἂν τοῖς χρωμέναις αὐτῇ
κατὰ συμβόλαια συνώκησεν, εἰ μήπερ
εὐθὺς ἐν τῷ πρώτῳ φωραθεῖσα ἀπώλετο.
Τῶν ΔΙΩΝΟΣ 'Ρωμαϊκῶν βιβλίον Ξ. [49]

Now Claudius left one day for Ostia at the mouth of the Tiber where he had completed the jetty and lighthouse begun by Caesar. He had excavated a port for corn from Africa, and fruits from Spain, Gaul and the Orient, to offer them in the temple of Castor, son of Tyndarus, who drives away pirates and storms—a single storm being capable of creating a food shortage in Rome.

Eight Liburnians carried him in a litter on the route, short and easy by horse—now twisting through forests of fig-trees and mulberries, now straight across flat open fields—but scarcely passable for carriages as it was unpaved for its entire length.

Learned in all things, save his own household, and reclining at length on his parasoled couch, he took it into his head to make himself illustrious in emulation of Cadmus, Cecrops, Linus, Palamedes, Simonides, Damaratus and Evander, and he invented three new letters for the alphabet: the eolic ⅃ [digamma] ; the)([anti-sigma] and a new dipthong which was to be the onomatapoeic representation of a kiss, that double fate.

In Rome, the consent of the prospective husband and wife, and of those on whom they were dependant, was all that was required for a marriage. The nuptial ceremonies were accessory.

But a wife became subject to the *paternal* authority of her husband, under his guardianship, and became his *property* like any other object, in three ways: by *usu, coemptione, farre.*

By *coemptione*: the husband bought her, with some formalities of fictitious emancipation, like an object.

By *confarreation*: This was the manner of union which Messalina chose, in the presence of ten witnesses, between the hands of the sovreign pontiff and flamen of Jupiter, κατὰ τοὺς ἱεροὺς νόμους. [50] And a cake of the grain called *far* was sacrificed to the gods.

Simultaneously Claudius was praying to Castor, protector of grains, that there might be no shortage of *far* in Rome.

Confarreation was an indissoluble union, with no possibility of divorce. It was a long ceremony which a clap of thunder, an unlucky omen, could nullify; but Castor granted Caesar's prayer.

Silius had divorced Junia Silvana the day before.

As for Messalina, wedded *for life* to Silius, she did not renounce her union with Caesar, nor desire the death of Claudius.

The mass murderess felt indulgence in her heart, infinite enough for generosity, toward all her former lovers, and recognised widowhood only as that calender convenience, denounced by Seneca, of dating by successive husbands instead of by consulates. For a woman, learned through wantonness, is more able to recall the names of her husbands than those of all the consuls: some of whom are dead, or far distant, or eunuchs—and they are all double.

And so she convinced herself quite sincerely that it was the lover of the moment that constituted her legitimate husband, and took steps to celebrate in the same manner, in the sequence of her future loves, but without renouncing their predecessors, a plurality of just and indissoluble nuptials.

Impunity crowned the first.

It was the end of Autumn. Consequently, to mock the seasons, symbol of the successive unity of husbands (according to prejudice), with a mean reversal, she imagined nothing better than to soak the wrinkled skins of the last grapes and redden the cheeks of the imperial palace in an imitation of the vintage, in honour of her marriage, and of Bacchus, ward of Priapus.

The nuptial couple, dressed in goat-skins, were surrounded by young elms in tubs, their branches bowed by clusters of grapes, by the dancing and singing of the slaves disguised as Bacchantes, and the sound of the wine-presses, groaning until they spurted blood. Messalina, dishevelled, was shaking a thyrsus; they felt the incense of the wine kiss their cothurni, and then fill their heads, until everything took on the disordered abandon of a roundelay, like gods rejoicing at the circling of the suns.

And this gyrating mass of people, more jumbled than the crushing grapes, was made up of all the former lovers of the bride, up to the present husband. From Mnester as Pan, clad in a wolf-skin, to the prostitute Cesoninus, a beardless Bacchus crowned with ivy, with whom Messalina had once tried to prove herself male.

All save Narcissus, their doyen, who had absented himself due to a sudden, ill-timed jealousy, the nuptial act only now appearing real to his secretarial nature, since it was in writing.

Vectius Valens, in a drunken sally, feigned to fly up and catch the

59

escaping ascension of the wine fumes which, under the pretext of rising to crown the gods, had robbed the drinker's brows of their nimbi; he climbed up the highest elm, and in the tones of an astrologer delimiting a celestial mansion, he cried;

'Eolus invites himself to the grape harvest; I can see a furious tempest approaching from Ostia!'

Thereupon the racket redoubled, with the multiple hilarity of the throbbing copper of the drums.

Wisely, he looked away from the sky, and observed the terrestial spectacle on the improvised stage of naked soil across which the last dead vineleaves were swept up in the flurry of the dance, as their heels beat the air, they imagined, in their drunkeness, that they were still crushing grapes.

There was a trembling among the vine-branches, like an elephant clearing a passage with its dark proboscis, laying low the grasses of Asia which are high trees; and an Ethiopian, naked as pitch, leapt forward following his satyric gesture.

His hands were bound behind his head, his elbows forming monstrous pierced ears instead of goat's horns. And so he had free use of but one member, acreted like a fighting cock, with a steel spur.

And, following a common practise of the Ethiopians, a small silver bell was encysted up to its sordine in the extremity of his skin; which did not prevent it clattering louder to Messalina's ear than all the bells of all the mules of all the teams yoked together to draw a battering ram up towards a city's gate.

Meanwhile the white gladiator leant against a young elm, outlined against the purple of the grapes, like a pearl rending the ear it adorns. He put himself on guard with masterly deliberation, with the dignity of a crucifixion.

Now, because the white was handsome, and the certain victor, Messalina felt herself becoming amorous of the negro.

And while all the women, even Cesoninus, and Silius and all the guests, encouraged one or the other antagonist with evocations of lust or derision, she leant without a word against one of the wine-stems around the arena, which bellied almost to breaking—her goat's feet stained to the ankles with the grapes' homage—and behind the negro, who could not see her, her eyes converged the ardent mirrors of her desire upon the white gladiator.

And because she was an expert and irresistable prostitute, and the other was only a male, Messalina's stare was not accorded the immediate riposte of a mere look, but of complete possession—the whole-hearted gift of an entire soul.

Having only a disarmed man to conquer, and because the Manes [51] rejoice in blood, the negro was permitted to kill.

But Messalina requested the sword of a professional executioner; so the killing would be swift.

'She is in haste,' thought Silius, 'for our nuptial couch, when the celebration ends.'

But after the man was dead: 'Kill!' the Empress repeated.

'Bacchus blinds you,' they all said to her, indicating the proof still lying before her, and the pool of blood that had not issued from the wine-presses.

'Kill!' said Messalina, paying no more attention to Silius, and addressing the negro more langorously than the wives of Tiberius asked for the single caress of his poisoned finger-nail: 'Quickly, kill me!'

The black butcher, in a stupor and confused, detached the cutting spur.

'He is a good negro, who knows how to stay alive,' Silius tried to laugh, to make the witnesses of his marriage forget a little that he was a husband, and contemplated dismissing Titius Proculus, the officer whom he had set to watch over his wife, or more exactly the *chamberlain of the heart* of Messalina.

'No, it would be too long,' Messalina sighed. 'Alone you would be more, you would be too much, oh my only lover!'

V

THE MULLET FISHERMAN

Λαίμαργος δὲ μάλιστα τῶν ἰχθύων ὁ
κεστρεύς ἐστι καὶ ἄπληστος· — ὅταν δὲ
φοβηθῇ, κρύπτει τὴν κεφαλήν, ὡς ὅλον
τὸ σῶμα κρύπτων.

ΑΡΙΣΤΟΤΕΛΟΥΣ Περὶ τὰ Ζῶα
ἱστοριῶν Η, 6. [52]

This occured at Nimes the same day that the Empress followed her last slave to the house of Caius Silius in Rome—now a whole city of adulteries, following her example.

On the beach still possessed by the Mediteranean, the physician Vectius Valens, sheltered by the wide brim of a Thessalanian hat like those worn by spectators at theatres or by sea-fishermen, pondered over a basket of fish.

Their grey, leaden backs gleamed, so broad the beasts were almost cylindrical; their bellies lolling, dull as a length of ivory cuirassed with metal—seven grey niellos rayed their flanks.

The heads, circled by a collar of four strong spines and with barbed gills, were prodigous: slanted and caparisoned in polygonal scales; the eyes were half covered by a double portico of spectacles composed of fat; the mouth with heavy lips, triangular and closing neatly like the impression of a die—Vectius opened one with his finger-nail, and this wriggling lip observed him in place of the dead eyes, the thin teeth blinked exactly like eye-lashes.

'The fisherman praised his merchandise, according to their varieties: the *cephalic, golden* and *leaping* mullets, and the tiny *labeo* mullet, and since the physician was absorbed in his examination yet appeared to have no intention of buying:

'I am still awaiting the ocean mullets!' he said, 'but here are the boats coming in now. You can watch the end of the fishing for *chelo* and *ramodo*.'

A small boat propelled by sail and oar appeared, hastening alone to the point where the speakers stood, at the end of the bay where the great salt pond *Latera* opened and communicated with the sea.

'They've been trailing a male mullet on a line by the mouth and gills for several days in the Atlantic,' the man explained, 'and the shoal of females follows blindly, for the mullet is both salacious and stupid.'

'Nature mocks the mullet,' said Vectius, 'they bury their heads in their fins, and think themselves hidden.'

'You're a fisherman?' the fisherman asked in surprise.

Vectius was looking out to sea.

The boats were all in view, but in no apparent order, and they did not seem to be forming a crescent or spreading nets across the bay.

And, whiter than the sails, the boiling froth of the wave-crests preceded them.

It was an advance-guard of dolphins, now visible on the surface of the water, herding the mullets like a pack of hounds.

'Mullets flee from dolphins, though they readily leap over a ship,' explained the fisherman.

A great crowd of men and women ran across the beach and the banks of the narrow entrance to the pond; they caught the entire shoal with tridents and hand-nets, for it was trapped in the shallows. The dolphins were unconcerned and frolicked nearby.

'They are waiting for their reward,' said the fisherman, 'and will stay here all night until they receive their usual payment—bread soaked in wine.'

Then he returned to his streaming baskets and began again:

'They're all exquisite to eat, for the sharp angle of their mouths only allows them to feed on soft animals, and their gullet acts as a filter and it is only the smaller particles that reach their stomachs.'

'You may add, friend, that the digestive process in that stomach is an infinitely subtle process, for it terminates in a bird's gizzard.'

'Are you buying at last—or are you a fisherman?' grumbled the mullet-man.

'I'm a fisherman, yes, in a way. I need neither sea nor hounds, nor even an abundance of fish. In Rome,' announced the physician, adjusting his Thessalanian hat, 'I remove the mullets of legal executions from the back-sides of adulterers.' [53]

VI

BY THE MEDIATION OF THE COURTESANS

Π ροανηρήκει δὲ τὴν γυναῖκα Μεσσαλίναν
διὰ ζηλοτυτίαν.
ΦΛ. ΙΟΣΗΦΟΥ 'Ιουδ. 'Αρχαιολογίας
βιβλ. Κ, κεφ. Ζ. 54

Now at Ostia, Claudius had been fully informed of all that had occured by Narcissus, and by Calpurnia and Cleopatra, his favourite concubines, and he was asking in confusion whether it was he or Silius that was Caesar.

This crazed perplexity left little room for a sentiment almost unknown it seems, among the Romans of that time, and least of all to Claudius—jealousy, hatred of being cuckolded; although Flavius Josephus claimed Claudius ordered the execution of Messalina from motives of jealousy.

'You're laughing at me, my little Cleopatra,' he stammered. 'Do not mock mê, I am only a poor man in a tavern. You want me to believe I am no longer Caesar! But you cannot take from Caesar, his palace, his treasures, his power and Venus, just like that! I still have all my reason, Calpurnia, I am very wise. You're still trying to place your muddy little shoes on my hands (there are people in my house who do not regard me as their master!) but you are wasting your time; I'm not asleep. My eyes are not dazzled. I have never been Caesar! The idea is too absurd!

He started.

'Torches! Blood! Friend soldier, here are pieces, many pieces of gold. You have good shoulders, soldier! Push the wheel! Push! *Io triumphe! Fors-Fortuna!*'

'Caesar,' began Narcissus—it was he who had entered.

'Ha ha! Caesar!' said Claudius, 'is it not so, Narcissus, *that it is not I!*'

'Why no,' the familiar agreed. 'Caesar is Caesar in Fortune's house. She is there, her chariot already harnessed and ready to leave.'

'She is there . . . *Venus?*' Caesar trembled in every limb.

'She awaits you . . .*Fors Fortuna*, Caesar.'

And in the same chair that had brought him to Ostia, between Vitellius and Largus Cecina, under Narcissus' eye, Claudius Caesar took the sandy road back to Rome.

Meanwhile *Venus*, came to meet him, but in a dung-cart, like garden refuse, for she had been unable to requisition any other vehicle, though as the *Augusta* she had as much right to a chariot as the goddess Livia. She was fearless, knowing that to blind the imperial eyes to the cartful of her crimes, she had only to open the voluptuous fan of her own.

And following the tradition of the *imaginary* soldier, that all creatures that bear the image of the monarch are invulnerable,[55] she brought with her their children, Octavia and Britannicus, who resembled Claudius even if he might not be their father.

Finally, as cynically as when she depilated herself, on her nights of prostitution, with a lamp sacred to the vestal virgins, she had herself preceded by Vibidia, the oldest of that order.

'Oh such crimes!' Cecina and Vitellius breathed alternately in each of Claudius' great ears, as though keeping the rhythm of the bearer's panting.

Narcissus, half-stretched out facing the Emperor, more cunningly called to Claudius' attention a memorial which revealed all Messalina's past, this spoke to the depths of his soul.

'A memorial?' said Claudius, avidly rummaging among his papers.

Last descendant of the noble family of Messalla and of centuries of integrity and rostra, daughter of Messalla the bearded and Domitia Lepida the Sweet Subduer, Messalina, whether Claudius had married her tarnished or not, and whether Lepida had made her an example of debauchery or virtue, had only curbed her infamy until she could with confidence rebel against the very summit of the Empire.

And after that, murders after murders.

Julia, Claudius' niece.

Julia, Claudius' sister.

Appius Silanus, second husband of Lepida, Messalina's mother whom her daughter had made a widow.

The sons of Appius, whom Claudius had hoped to make his sons-in-law.

Claudius' son-in-law, Pompey the Great, and his father, and his mother.

Callistus, fellow-student and freedman of Claudius.

Vicinius Quartinus.

Pelius and Anna, famous . . .

Claudius, tired of murders, turned for distraction to the roll of exiles.

Seneca . . .

From the bloody bottom of this infamous stew he did not raise his head to the more dangerous pestilence in the dung-cart.

VII

ATROPUS IN THE GARDENS OF LUCULLUS

Et vincula, et carcerem, et tormenta, et
supplicia [miles] administrabit, nec suarum
erit ultor injuriarum? Iam stationes aliis
magis faciet quam Christo?
Q. SEPT. FLOR. TERTULLIANI *De Corona*[56]

Now the widowed matron took pity on the guilty child, certain she was to be punished, and she went to comfort the unhappy one who had taken refuge behind the iron gates of the gardens—a vain opposition to the approaching iron of the soldiers.

As for her accomplices, the Emperor automatically, and nonchalantly, ordered their execution. Being an antiquary in love with old customs, Claudius had said merely:

'Punish them *in the ancient manner.*'

Since all the ancient practices of Latium were bloody, this order signified: Put them to death. The traditional methods of execution included: beating to death with rods, or beating with rods followed by beheading, or being thrown from the Tarpeian rock—though this punishment was generally reserved for parricides. But surely the Emperor was a father, just as in Roman matrimonial law, he was father to his wife, Messalina? One might also be strangled in the Tullianum or Force prisons.

Silius claimed his right to the block, in heroic rodomontades; Vectius Valens was garrulous; Mnester enveloped himself in a cloak of cowardly supplications, indicating, with great ostentation, the scars inflicted on Caesar's orders in the cavern of Diana Persia.

'They are unimportant,' said Claudius. 'I have ordered the beheading of a consul-designate and too many other nobles to make an exception of a mere histrion! Particularily as his name is ΜΝΗΣΤΗΡ, the Gallant; and this will provide me with a Homeric title for my account of his death in my history of Rome: Μνηστηροφονια,[57] the Massacre of the Gallants of . . . Penelope, which is the argument of Canto 22 of the Odyssey. Let him not escape execution or he will rob me of my title.'

The following was ocurring not far from the grotto of Diana:

"ttle, 'ttle girl . . . she has been a clever little girl! Mother, give me the little silver lamp so I can play at being a vestal?'

66

It was Messalina speaking. The garden gates had been broken down. Her sudden mortal terror, across the knees of Domita Lepida, anticipated the delirium of her agony.

'Very good! She'll never break the *futile* by using it as a spinning top!'

A *futile* was the sacred vessel employed to sprinkle the temple of Vesta, its base, in order that not a drop of water remained in it, was conical in shape like a soda bottle.

'Give me the lamp of the youngest vestal!'

And then, preceded by a centurian in guards uniform, less fatal and inflexible in his weapons than in his military silence, came Evodus carrying a torch. He inundated the lawn with the crude illumination of his slave's insults.

Lepidus drew her widow's veil across her face.

'Bitch, she-wolf, whore!' shouted the freedman and, save for the sudden barking of orders to his soldiers, he did not interrupt his ranting and insults until his mission was accomplished.

'A soldier!' lisped Messalina, 'there's a soldier. Someone has caressed me with soldier's words! Mother, let me go to the beautiful soldiers!'

'Please?'

She groped at the face, taciturn under its mask of white crumbcloth.

' . . . the veil. Why, the Augustan god is veiled!' [58]

Joyfully:

'Good, good! The great gladiator is going to slit the little one's throat! Lift me in your arms, mother, so the young boys with their golden bulla can admire me with my thumbs clasped together.'

The freedman became impatient.

'It is useless to feign madness, o most abject of adulteresses! Comedian, you are not in the Circus! Your cuckold of a Caesar has decided at last to mete out justice and nothing can save you. Tribune of the guard, advance.'

The tribune, his medals and *phalerae* swinging on his chest, advanced into the gaze of Messalina.

The centurians and soldiers were frequently charged with executions. Tertullian, describing their various duties, exclaimed:

'What! He must administer irons and prison, torture and punishments, and yet he cannot avenge his own wrongs? And he is to mount guard more over others than over Christ?' [59]

'My dear,' said Messalina, she scanned him from head to foot, still at length on her veiled mother's lap. 'I love you. I was so eager to love you that I did not waste *our* time in turning to look at you. For now, I'm happy in the knowledge that you're a soldier. You are beautiful, like a goatskin bottle in

67

your leather tunic! Smells good. I'm beautiful too, aren't I? The *leno* says I'm the most beautiful of all. The men call me Lycisca.'

'Silence, filth!' cried the freedman, 'your words affront even the name of the City's whores.'

She put a finger in her mouth, pensive and rebellious.

'Mother, as you have forbidden your little girl to walk in the Suburra— although Halotus says it is very lovely (there is a great tub there that the men pee in), lend me your little 'thyphallic bracelet for a plaything.'

Without breaking her mournful silence the matron stood up brusquely and pressed a dagger into her daughter's hand, she had clasped it since before the arrival of the executioners.

The reality of the metal recalled Messalina to her senses, she reawakened, imperious.

'I was dreaming! I was mad! Yes, die, and wash away all this shame . . . But, idiot servant, this bath is too cold, you deserve to be pricked with the golden needle. Where am I? The gardens?'

She fell to her knees.

'Phales! He's gone! Flying away, smaller, ever smaller . . . I'll never catch him! Cottyto, you'll be rewarded for recovering my jewel. That little coral and sardonyx brooch which holds together my embroidered robe. Oh my little fledgling return to your nest, pretty murrhine, frothing little cup, Sili!'

'Enough nonsense,' growled Evodus. 'I suspect that at this very moment your lover is vomiting his crimes in blood. Perhaps if your mouth was permitted to drink his soul, it would prevent it escaping elsewhere, close up all his wounds with your fingers, o viler than baladines and flute-players!'

'Ah, do not hurt Silius. The melody of my kisses will be the same with seven lovers, without hurting him. O Pan! O Syrinx!'[60]

She gently stroked her throat with the stiletto.

'She's delirious. On your knees, slut! Tribune, draw your blade!'

And slowly the soldier began to draw the first inches of the heavy sword.

Messalina, at the flash of steel, dropped her dagger and clapped her hands.

'Yes, the soldier's, the soldier's! Claudi, beloved, stop, it's for me to undress you! You are beautiful because you're old, old and bald, so bald that nothing could be more naked! Or uglier, o my lover! Where the ugliness of man terminates, in his paroxysm, there exactly is the beginning of the flower's beauty. Come, lily of the gardens! My Emperor!'

She seized the long executioner's blade by the brilliant visible steel and drew out its entire length.

The freedman hesitated now.

'Stop, tribune. Perhaps she will kill herself. The secretary said it would be better if she did kill herself.'

The tribune let fall his arm but without releasing his grip on his sword, the sole useful, *infamous* finger of the military fist.

'Ah, how icy you are!' she said. 'Do not touch Messalina's heart all at once, for it is so soft there you would burn yourself, you're so cold. And besides, you would not love me if I didn't flirt a little! I want to refuse just long enough for you to be slightly less cold. Let my kisses warm you gradually.'

She laid her cheek against the steel, as though sleeping on her mirror.

'Woman,' said the freedman to Lepida, 'does your daughter know what she is saying?'

Lepida lowered her veil and looked, with the eye of Juno.

Messalina had rent the flimsy covering of her robe, and her breast was naked as the blade.

'Slut!' spat Evodus.

'What are you saying my great mirror? *Why do I admire my reflection, all naked?*'

Smiling at the blade, gleaming like a wet fish with striped flanks, waiting for its master to plunge it in:

'And you, do you bathe fully dressed?'

The tribune wrenched clumsily at his weapon, attempting to disengage it.

'Oh, don't leave me,' cried Messalina. 'Press yourself to me! Not so hard. Don't push yourself away with all your arms. Let me lift myself to your mouth.'

She raised herself towards the tribune.

'Ah, you are a god, PHALES! Phales, I knew nothing of Love; I knew all men but you are the first Immortal I have loved! Phales, at last, and so late! I knew you were in the garden; wicked, you sent me a mere actor in a mask! Such a heavy mask. But now, it's really you. Welcome! You have waited so long, Master. Let us go home. My mother isn't looking. She's only the widow of a great bearded one, she doesn't understand. It's really you. I've not been dreaming, or am I dreaming now?'

Evodus, stupidly:

'She dreams, or at least pretends to.'

Messalina, joyfully, to the blade:

'Welcome!'

And the steel monster answered her kiss with a bite, just above her breast, which was a prelude to its possessing her entirely.

'Carry me away, Phales! The apotheosis, I want it immediately, before I become old! O make me old now, as old as the gods. Take me away to our home in the highest heavens! The highest? The first! You are the first, O Immortal! You can see that I'm a virgin! Give me the lamp so I can play at being a little vestal. So virginal! So late! Happiness, how you hurt! Kill me, Happiness! Death! give me . . . the little lamp of death. I'm dying . . . I knew all along one could only die of love! I have it . . . mother!'

The man with the sword thrust Messalina from him as he would a viper.

She stretched her fumbling hands towards Lepida who, without haste, stole away. The matron replaced her veil and retreated, walking backwards.

'But it's a blade, carrion,' foamed the freedman, 'not . . .'

Now he burst into sobs and was prostrated as though by the blasting exhalation of a god; and his bites nestled among the flowers whose perfumes exalted with his cry:

'But I love her!'

And from beneath the flowers he gasped toward the hope of a woman's face. None. The widow had gone, grave and pitiless. She was so much a widow, so pure and pitiless, she had not been there for some time. And that which raised up and animated the immaculate hood was perhaps nothing else but the Divine Obscenity which had withdrawn to the secret places of his garden. Only a god or a phantom could have arranged the folds so perfectly. A real woman would have wept before the slave did, and her face would have been disclosed by the cloth, moulded to it by her tears.

The god had departed.

There was no one left in His gardens but the tribune and Messalina; and the woman, as the steel was slowly withdrawn, sank toward the limitless void of the flowers.

The tribune extracted the entire blade, paused, and concluded:
'Whore!'

VIII

APOCOLOCYNTOSIS[61]

Inter cetera in eo mirati sunt homines
et oblivionem et inconsiderantiam, vel,
ut graece dicam, μετεωριαν et εξλεψιαν
Occisa Messalina, paulo post, quam in
triclinio decubuit, 'cur domina non
veniret', requisivit.
C. SUETONII TRANQUILI *Tib. Claud.* XXXIX.[62]

Messalina is dead.' said Narcissus.

Claudius was eating, half asleep, on his dining couch.

'She is beautiful, she is amorous, she is dead, she is Venus,' he repeated in a toneless voice. 'Go and tell her to come and join us at table. She is beautiful, I love her, I am happy.'

'She is dead,' said Narcissus.

'Dead, I undersatnd. She is very faithful. I have not embraced her this morning. Go, tell her to come, it is late.'

'The time of your meal has been put forward, Caesar.'

'The time put forward? Quite correct! I can always put time forward. That is why I am happy, knowing she is not late. She is not in pain, I know. I am so contented. Call her.'

Narcissus touched Claudius' shoulder and threw across the couch a red-stained under-tunic.

'She is dead. At last do you understand?'

At the sight of blood the wide nostrils of the Emperor quivered.

'The moon? I had forgotten, forgive me, Narcissus; my nature is becoming somewhat . . . meteoric and ableptic! Soon I shall be more ignorant of what is happening to the planets than the people of Taprobana, who can only see the moon above the earth in the second week of each month. You are a good calender, Narcissus. I have understood. But I want my wife to join me at table even so. I am hungry, and yet satiated—with happiness.'

'Caesar?'

'She is dead, I know. Women play at being murdered at each new moon.'

'You no longer have a wife, Caesar! Yesterday, you said they were all to be massacred, you did not specify, even the actor was unimportant, she was no exception. She has been stabbed and is no longer, the Senate has just ordered the removal of her name and image from the public places and in particular from your palace and this room, Caesar.'

'So . . . *Venus* . . . is no longer?'

And with a maniacal gesture, he inverted his great cup and slammed it down on the ringing silver plate which covered the whole serving table, and he listened to the gradual descent of the silence.

He listened with all the anguish of one of the Danaides,[63] bent over her torment. And without transition, he burst into uncontrollable laughter, and eyes alight with a divine hope, he thrust the same goblet at the cup-bearer:

'A DRINK.'

And it was then that Claudius Caesar—propped on one elbow on his couch, insatiable for love and feasting, pale, his cheek cerulean from the recent assiduity of his barber, a prototype Bluebeard just a few generations on from the cynocephalus, ancestor of our glorious warriors—meditated on his fourth wife:

Agrippina.

FINIS

NOTES & SOURCES

1. **The House of Happiness:** The chapter title derives from a celebrated inscription found in Pompei above a shop doorway—'Hic habitat felicitas' accompanied by a phallus. There is no evidence that the shop was other than a bakery.

2. From Juvenal, **Satires,** VI, lines 129-32. '. . . she stayed till the end, always the last to go, then trailed away sadly, still with a burning hard-on, retiring exhausted, yet still far from satisfied . . .' Much of this chapter derives from this source.

3. **Ruminal:** Pliny's **Natural History,** XV 310, states 'In the Forum a fig-tree is carefully cultivated (...) as a memorial of the fig-tree which in former days over-shadowed Romulus and Remus in the Lupercal cave. This tree received the name—**rumialis**' from the circumstance that under it the wolf was found giving the breast—**rumis** it was called in those days—to the two infants.'

4. **Lares:** Lares Praestites, the good spirits of the City of Rome.

5. **Pan:** Jarry combines the Greek Pan (half-goat) with the Roman Faun.

6. From Pliny, **Natural History,** X, 82, in which Messalina is the victor.

7. **Pretext:** purple-bordered toga worn by magistrates.

8. Prudentius, **Against Symmachus,** I, 219; translated in the text 'Her worship is bloody, etc.' p. 19.

9. The list of Claudius' works is from Suetonius, **Claudius,** 4; although Jarry combines the treatise on dice and the autobiography. Suetonius, together with Tacitus, **Annals,** IX, and Cassius Dio Lx are the main sources on Claudius.

10. There is no note 10.

11. The Greek proverb put in Claudius' mouth is from Seneca, **The Apocolocyntosis of the Divine Claudius,** 1. Theoginus is presumed to be a famous idiot of the time.

12. **Senes:** from 'senio', six.

13. **Hephaestus:** Vulcan, the god of fire, the lame and deceived husband of Venus.

14. **Lituus:** augural wand.

15. **Templum:** area delineated by ritual for prophecy.

16. **Hermaeum:** 'Hermes-room', dining-room.

17. **Spina:** central wall of the Circus Maximus.

18. From Plutarch, **On the Disappearance of Oracles,** 17, in which it is interpreted as predicting the end of paganism.

19. **Cynobellinus:** Ancient king of the Britons; **Camulodunum** is thought to be Colchester or Maldon. This and the following anecdote are from Cassius Dio, LX,19-22 & 51-56, although here the legions are called 'Claudian, Loyal and Patriotic'.

20. **Pallium:** cloak; **Xysti:** promenade lined with trees.

21. Columella, **On Agriculture,** X (on horticulture), V 31-34, 'As a trunk of an old rough-hewn tree, the divinity of the Ithyphallus is venerated in the form of a terrible member, which, in the middle of gardens, menaces the urchins with its sex, and shakes its scythe'.

22. This sentence, and other details, derive from Cassius Dio, LXI, 30. The remaining account of the trial of Valerius is from Tacitus, XI, 1-3. Jarry deliberately gives Valerius Chinese characteristics, an impossibility in Rome at this time. The family of Valerius originated in Asia Minor. Jarry also takes advantage of the identical French spelling (Vienne) of Vienna, and Vienne, a town on the Rhone, and Valerius' birth-place.

23. **Amometus:** third century Greek author, whose principal work **On the Attacors,** is lost. The Attacors were a fabled race from the furthest Orient (cf. Pliny, VI, 39).
Dioscurias, a prosperous trading place in central Asia (Pliny, VI, 6).

24. Chop-sticks!

25. 'Be first to attack him who would attack you', Homer, **Iliad,** XXIV, 369.

26. **The Apollo:** name of Lucullus' dining-room. Plutarch says Lucullus was disabled by

the potion, not killed by it; however, Pliny, XXV, 8, records he died of it. **Atropus:** one of the three fates–**Clotho,** spins the thread of life, **Lachesis,** determines its length, **Atropus,** cuts it.

27. Plutarch, **Lucullus,** 39: 'In so much that even now, with all the advance of luxury, the Lucullean gardens are counted the noblest the Emperor has.'

28. Cassius Dio, LX, 22, states Mnester was 'on intimate terms' with Caligula, a phrase open to various interpretretations.

29. **Nephilibates:** 'Cloud-riders', a word invented by Rabelais, IV, 56; **Mantichores** make frequent appearances in Jarry's works. Pliny, VIII, 30, records that it was a native of Ethiopia and was particularily fond of human flesh, they look like this:

30. Tacitus, **Annals,** VI, 28, 'During the consulate of Paullus Fabius and Lucius Vitellius, at the conclusion of an age-long cycle, the phoenix appeared in Egypt . . . it's first function, on reaching adulthood is the burial of its father . . . it takes up its father's body, and carries it to the altar of the sun, and burns it'.

31. **Pale:** in the heraldic meaning of the word.

32. Pliny, **Natural History,** XXXVII, 8, 'Murrhines come from the Orient. Many types exist, the least remarkable are found in the country of the Parthians. The most beautiful are found in Carmania. They are thought to be a humour which is condensed underground'.

33. **Auriga:** chariot-driver.

34. Suetonius, **Caligula,** 54, chapter title is translation. The obelisk appearing in this chapter is described in Pliny XXXVI, 15, and is now in the place of the Cathedral of St.Peter in Rome.

35. This anecdote is from Cassius Dio, LX, 28.

36. **Caius:** or Gaius, i.e. Caligula, the anecdotes in Mnester's songs derive from Suetonius.

37. **Amphion:** Amphion and Zethus, children of Zeus, fortified Thebes–Zethus, with his great strength, brought up stones, Amphion, a harper of more than mortal skill, fitted them together with the music of his lyre.

38. Cassius Dio, LX, 26, records that an eclipse, occurring on Claudius' birthday and being interpreted as an evil omen, prompted Claudius to publish an explanatory treatise. Dio's account of its contents is here put into Claudius' mouth verbatim.

39. **Glomeramen:** from Lucretius, **The Nature of the Universe,** V, 726.

40. Pliny, **Natural History,** XXVII, 28, 'Thus for instance, upon the Latin festival, it is the custom to have a race of four-horsed chariots in the Capital, and for the conqueror to be presented with a draught of wormwood'.

41.**Burdigala:** Bordeaux; **Taprobana:** Ceylon.

42. Cassius Dio, LX, 22, reports that Messalina tricked Claudius into ordering Mnester to do whatever she requested, and Mnester therefore, believed he was indulgent towards her adultery. Claudius' fear of assasination at table (next para.) is in Suetonius, **Claudius,** 35. Jarry manages a dig at the army, always one of his favourite targets.

43. Apart from Jarry's personal researches into the properties of absinthe, this information comes from Pliny, XXVII, 28; XIV, 19, describes the manufacture of **pthorium;** XXV, 36, states that **Artemisia** is **similar** to wormwood; and **hippomane,** according to VIII, 66, is a poisonous substance derived from the foreheads of newly-born horses, and employed in philtres.

44. **Ink:** ibid. XXVII, 28.

45. Chapter title is translation.

46. From Cassius Dio, LX, 17, Jarry was a Breton.

47. **Odyssey,** XXIII, 202-3, 'And I know not, wife, whether our bed still stands inviolate'.

48. On the 23rd of January, the Catholic Church celebrates St. Messalina, virgin and martyr. She died in 250, her relics, recovered in 1599, provoked miracles and she was canonized in 1613 by Paul V!! **Ab-so-lutely:** in French 'ab-solu-ment', when spoken is a pun 'absolute lie'.

49. Cassius Dio, LXI, 31, 'And she would have been married by a legal contract to all those who enjoyed her favours, had she not been detected and destroyed on her very first attempt'.Other sources for this chapter: On Claudius' invention of letters, Tacitus, XI, 13, and Pliny VII, 57; on his public works, Suetonius, **Claudius,** 20; on Messalina's marriage, Tacitus, XI, 31; on confarreation, Pliny, XVIII, 3.

57. 'According to the sacred laws', Seneca, **De beneficiis,** III, 16.

58. **Manes:** spirits of the dead.

52. Aristotle, **Natural History of the Animals,** VIII, 2, 'Of all the fish, the mullet is the most voracious and the most insatiable . . . When frightened, they hide their heads, believing their whole body is hidden.' Pliny, IX, 8-17, provides most of the information on mullets and their methods of capture. Jarry reverses the male and female roles in this process, however.

53. From Juvenal, **Satires,** X, 315-17, 'And sometimes an outraged cuckold will go far beyond all legal sanctions and horsewhip his rival to ribbons, stab him through the heart, or stick a mullet up his backside'!

54. Flavius Josephus, **Antiquities of the Jews,** XX, 7, 'He made his wife Messalina kill herself, through jealousy'. Jarry repeats the anecdote from Suetonius of shoes being placed on Claudius' hands while he was asleep and drunk (see p. 16). The sources for this chapter (including Claudius' confusion over whether he was Caesar or not, and Messalina's using a dung-cart) are Tacitus, XI, 31; Suetonius, **Claudius,** 36.

55. From Vegetius, **Epitome Rei Militaris,** II, 7.

56 Translated in text, see note 59. **Atropus:** see note 26. On Messalina's death, Dio, LXI, 31, reports '(Claudius) then slew Messalina herself after she had retreated into the gardens of Asiaticus' he then adds enigmatically—'which more than anything else were the cause of her ruin'.

57. **Mnesterophonia:** The massacre of the pretenders.

58. The veiling of the Augustan statue indicates the imminence of death (see p. 16).

59. This paragraph is the translation of the quote at the head of the chapter.

60. **Syrinx:** An Arcadian Nymph, daughter of the river god Ladon; she was changed by her sisters into a reed in her flight from the enamoured Pan. Pan cut this reed into seven pieces, and joined them together with wax, in gradually decreasing lengths to form the

instrument known as a 'syrinx' or 'Pan's-pipe'.

61. **Apocolocyntosis:** literally 'Pumpkinification'; it is the title of Seneca's satire on Claudius' ascent to heaven, his treatment there by all those he has murdered and his final punishment, to perpetually attempt to throw dice from a bottomless dice-cup.

62. Suetonius, **Claudius,** 39, 'Claudius' scatter-brainedness and shortsightedness—or if you prefer the Greek terms, his **meteoria** and **ablepsia**—were truly remarkable. Having executed Messalina , he went in to dinner, and after a while asked 'Why is her ladyship not present?''.

63. **Danaides:** daughters of Danau, condemned for the murders of their husbands, to pour water for ever into vessels with holes in their bottoms.

ALSO AVAILABLE FROM ATLAS PRESS

THE MAGNETIC FIELDS by *ANDRE BRETON & PHILIPPE SOUPAULT*. A masterly translation by *DAVID GASCOYNE* of the first work in the Surrealist canon.

ATLAS ANTHOLOGY TWO. Texts, chiefly prose by *QUENEAU, BRETON, PERET, JARRY, DAUMAL, ARTMANN, BAYER, PANIZZA, VIAN, PEREC, ROUSSEL, RINGELNATZ, FLESCH-BRUNNINGEN, SATIE, GASCOYNE, BLEGVAD, MATHEWS, JENKINS*.

FORTHCOMING

ATLAS ANTHOLOGY THREE texts by *BRETON, QUENEAU, JARRY, PEREC, MATHEWS, KIRKUP, BLEGVAD, BRUS, JENKINS, PERET, PANIZZA, GASCOYNE, RIGAUT, WAINHOUSE, MEYRINK, ARTMANN, BAYER, BRISSET, JONES, ROUSSEL, WALSER, VIAN, LINCOLN, SHIEL, SCHEERBART, SCHWITTERS, BAUER, KRAUS, PASOLINI, ROSENDORFER, ALBERT-BIROT, ZURN*, et al.

PATAPHYSICAL SYLLOGES, SOLILOQUIES, COLLOQUIES AND SUPERCOLLUVIES by *ALFRED JARRY*. Jarry's own selection from his contributions to periodicals. Thirty-odd, odd exegeses of black humour and the 'science of imaginary solutions'.

THE ATLAS ANTHOLOGY OF KONRAD BAYER. We hope to be publishing, late in 1986, the first definitive English selection of the works of this major Austrian author, a delimiter of universals.

All available from:

ATLAS PRESS, 10 PARK STREET, LONDON SE1 9AB

Write for details, or to join our mailing list